The fireworks course

They set off fireworks the night you were born, Teresa. The doctor who worked over you was so quick and sure that you were soon lying quietly. He just hadn't let there be time for anything to go wrong. I was mad at him, though. He wanted me to look after myself, stay away and rest and leave you to the nurse, but all I wanted was to be with you, so I made up mind that I'd fight him if I had to. I was ready to do anything for you, Teresa.

Even if it meant making an enemy of William Hartman, she decided with ruthless determination. As she went into her room at last, she could still feel the warm brushstrokes of his touch across her face.

After living in the USA for nearly eight years, **Lilian Darcy** is back in her native Australia with her American historian husband and their three young children. More than ever, writing is a treat for her now, looked forward to and luxuriated in like a hot bath after a hard day. She likes to create modern heroes and heroines with good doses of zest and humour in their make-up, and relishes the opportunity that the medical series gives her for dealing with genuine gripping drama in romance and in daily life. She finds research fascinating too—everything from attacking learned medical tomes to spending a day in a maternity ward.

Recent titles by the same author:

MIRACLE BABY

BY
LILIAN DARCY

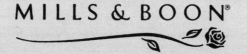

MILLS & BOON®

First published in Great Britain 1997
Harlequin Mills & Boon Limited,
Eton House, 18-24 Paradise Road, Richmond, Surrey TW9 1SR

© Lilian Darcy 1998

ISBN 0 263 80703 7

Set in Times 10 on 12 pt. by
Rowland Phototypesetting Limited
Bury St Edmunds, Suffolk

03-9803-48710-D

Printed and bound in Great Britain
by Mackays of Chatham PLC, Chatham

CHAPTER ONE

—They set off fireworks to celebrate your birth, Teresa.

That's what I'll tell her, Jennifer Powell vowed as she stared at the bright display from the window of the ninth floor at Riverbank Hospital.

Cascades of stars, like thistles or pompoms, exploded into the dark, smoky haze of the night sky—pink and green and amethyst, red, white and blue. It was Sunday night on the Fourth of July weekend, and the city of Columbus, Ohio, was celebrating.

Jennifer saw Dr William Hartman's approach reflected in the dark glass as a brief lull came in the pyrotechnic display and she turned, knowing what he had come to tell her.

'Dr Powell?'

'Mmm?' Her throat was tight with emotion, and she couldn't quite manage 'yes'.

His wide, firmly drawn mouth was set very soberly and there was a deep frown of concern etched above his dark eyes. 'I've just called Richard Gilbert,' he said. 'He's on his way in, and the maternity operating room staff downstairs are getting your sister prepped for the delivery. We'll have a baby within the hour.'

And my sister's life will end.

It would be the punctuation point to the longest weekend of Jennifer's existence. The events of the past three days crowded in upon her memory and she relived them as she followed Will Hartman's capable figure, thinking absently

that he looked as tired as she felt. Like her, he had spent
too many of the past forty-eight hours at the hospital.

On Friday morning she had had no inkling of this, had
never set foot in Riverbank—or Columbus, for that matter—in her life. On Friday morning she'd been rounding
in the paediatric unit of Massachusetts State University
Hospital in Boston—her fifth day as a first-year resident
in paediatrics.

On Friday morning, when she'd been called to the phone
at the nurse's station, she'd had no premonition that she
was about to hear the concerned yet formal voice of a
stranger, telling her that her sister, Heather, had been in a
serious accident in Columbus, Ohio, and was in surgery
now but was not expected to live.

She had been given compassionate leave at once. Alan
Brinkley, the doctor in charge of M.S.U.H.'s medical residency programme, was aware, from details in her personal
file, of her family situation. Parents in Hong Kong for
a year, adoptive sister whose whereabouts were currently
unknown. . .

She had booked a flight from the same phone at the
nurses' station, then had driven home to pack distractedly,
leaving her car and its keys with Tom Dane, her parents'
resident caretaker. He had been appalled at the news, of
course.

'Don't worry, Tom. I'll tell my parents. They—they
won't want to fly back, I expect.'

Then she had taken a taxi to the airport and had made
her flight with seconds to spare.

Another taxi driver at the Columbus end had rec-
ommended a motel. 'Yes, very near Riverbank Hospital,
and it has a pool.'

A pool? It hadn't even registered. She'd had the taxi

wait, checked in, flung her suitcase onto the bed and had been at the hospital five minutes later.

The gestational age of the baby that Heather was carrying had been the paramount thing. Somehow Jennifer had already accepted that her sister had reached the end of her own road. It had been a long time coming. Adopted at the age of two, after an appalling start in life, Heather had never been able to give her adoptive parents what they'd wanted.

What they'd wanted was another child like Jennifer—healthy, happy, bright and successful. Instead, Heather had grown up with a series of odd problems, both physical, mental and emotional, which had never been properly diagnosed despite the barrow-loads of Powell money flung in the direction of a dozen different specialists.

It hadn't been the right way to treat her, Jennifer knew. Heather hadn't needed specialists, she'd needed acceptance.

And so at twelve had begun the attempts at running away. By thirteen, Heather had been sexually active, at fifteen she'd garnered her first drug conviction and by sixteen she'd been on the streets and lost to sight for months at a time.

'I've washed my hands of her,' Julia Powell had declared, and had meant it. Her husband hadn't disagreed.

Jennifer, then nineteen, and well embarked on her pre-med courses at Harvard, had been able to retain her love for Heather, if not her optimism about Heather's future. *A year ago the only thing that surprised me was that she'd made it as far as she had,* she thought now.

When she'd arrived outside the intensive care unit late on Friday afternoon Jennifer had seen in the face of the nurse who'd answered the unit's buzzer that Heather had presented few surprises to the staff either.

They probably think there'll be drugs in her system, Jennifer had thought. Did they test for that, I wonder, at some point? Or hasn't there been time? But there *won't* be drugs. Heather wouldn't have done that, not when she's always blamed so many of her own problems on a drug-abusing mother!

'Will you wait out here?' the nurse had said to her. 'The team in charge of your sister's case is in consultation now, but someone will be available to talk to you soon.'

She had nodded and turned to the same windows from which the fireworks could now be seen, staring unseeingly out of them as she'd waited. On Friday there hadn't been fireworks, of course. Instead, the view she'd had had been of lines of speeding traffic in both directions along the freeway against a backdrop of humid haze. It had been just as meaningless, though, as tonight's shower of pretty stars.

And on Friday, as now, it had been Will Hartman who had come to talk to her. At the time he'd been just a stranger, just a voice mouthing the sort of phrases that she herself had used in her professional role—'Everything that could be done. . .condition is extremely critical. . .cautiously optimistic about the outlook for the baby's survival. . .'

He had been a name and a professional title, like a cardboard cut-out of a doctor, and she might have hated him if she'd spared any energy for anything other than grieving for Heather and hoping—*praying*—for the baby.

Slowly, though, over the past two days she had come to realise that, for good or ill, Will Hartman would for ever be much more to her than a stranger, a voice, a name. He was a part of this thing now, a key player in the drama that would stay fresh and sharp in her memory for the rest of her life.

And he had played his part well, too, she was able to perceive in hindsight. There had been genuine care in the way he'd talked to her, as if he'd really understand... almost as if he'd been through something like this himself... And when he had laid a hand for one long moment on her small shoulder she'd felt strengthened and grateful.

'Is there any chance that Heather will live?' she had demanded.

'I can't—' He'd cut off the words with a sigh. 'You're a doctor...'

'Just a first-year resident.'

'A *doctor*. You must shy away from pronouncing certainty and finality as much as I do. I'm a neonatologist. My concern is with the foetus. But I have to tell you that the trauma team is thinking of this the same way I am: what can we do for the mother to save the baby?' He'd hesitated. 'You'll know, perhaps, if that's what she would have wanted.'

'It is,' Jennifer had answered at once. 'Whatever else she may or may not have been, whatever she may have done in her life—*with* her life—she wouldn't have done anything to harm her baby. I saw her two months ago. She was even growing out her bleached hair rather than use dye. She wasn't smoking or drinking or doing drugs. She *wanted* to—she was quite wired, she told me, from cocaine withdrawal. She'd stopped taking it even before she conceived, apparently, so I think at some level she must have wanted to be pregnant...but she was staying strong.'

'Then the baby has a better chance now.'

'I know. I'm clinging to that...'

They had talked for a short while longer but he'd had to go down to the neonatal intensive care unit, and for the

rest of the weekend he'd just been an occasional presence—
one of a dozen other people at the periphery of her awareness, coming or going from Heather's bed in the ICU as
everyone fought to buy the tiny baby a few more precious
days in her mother's womb.

Several people had politely suggested that Jennifer go
to her motel and get some rest, but Will Hartman hadn't
been one of them. Computing the hours at which she'd
glimpsed him—three on Saturday morning, then again at
eleven and at four on Sunday afternoon—she'd known he
must be on call and having a brutal weekend of it. And all
the while, as everyone had expected, Heather was deter-
iorating.

They'd sent Jennifer out, finally, at about eight tonight—
Sunday night.

'You had breakfast at ten,' one of the nurses had said
accusingly. 'You're a slip of paper as it is. Get dinner
before the cafeteria closes if you won't leave the hospital
and go to a decent restaurant.'

Knowing she was right, Jennifer had gone for her meal,
and when she'd returned they'd said the team was in conference and they wouldn't let her in. Now it transpired that
Heather had already been taken downstairs.

'You came up just to get me?' she asked Dr
Hartman now.

He shrugged and smiled faintly. 'Didn't want you to
get lost.'

The humour was so gentle and so right that it was almost
her undoing, and as they entered the elevator she had to
lean against its bland walls to harness her strength enough
to stand.

He saw it too, and a fleeting frown of concern crossed
his face. He didn't comment, though, and she was grateful

for that. It was obvious that this was a nightmare for her, obvious that she was exhausted and should have tried to sleep and obvious that she was both too strong-willed and too concerned to give in to her body's need—which meant that both scoldings and expressions of sympathy were pointless.

The lift stopped at the eighth floor to admit a female doctor and then again at the seventh to allow her to exit, which gave Jennifer more time to flesh out her impression of the man who stood next to her.

He was strongly but not massively built, with square, capable shoulders. Tall enough to suggest a degree of arrogance, but not tall enough to allow deliberate intimidation—if intimidation had been his style, and she somehow felt it wasn't.

His facial features were uncompromisingly masculine yet capable of showing softness, too—the way his wide mouth had a tiny upward tuck at each corner, the way his chin made his bottom lip lift and curve when it jutted, the way his dark brows could arrow down towards the sharply delineated bridge of his nose or rise to stretch the fine skin of his eyelids and emphasise the thick length of his lashes.

'This is it,' he said when they reached the sixth floor. 'I'm. . .well, I've been assuming you want to be there for the delivery.'

'If I can.'

'The trauma team had some doubts. I. . .overrode them.'

'I should thank you, then.'

He shrugged a little. 'You're a doctor.'

'That's not why it's right for me to be there. She's going to be my baby.' They knew the sex from the ultrasound scan that had been done on Friday afternoon. 'I want to be present at the birth.'

'You'll adopt her?' He was trying to conceal... something. She couldn't tell. Surprise? Disapproval? Scepticism? It could have been anything.

'Yes.' She didn't want to elaborate, although she could have done. *My parents won't want her. There's no one else. This will probably ruin my career, but any other option is unthinkable.*

No, she definitely didn't want to elaborate.

'Finally, though, on the issue of your being present,' Dr Hartman was saying, 'it's up to Richard Gilbert.'

'Richard—?' For a moment her mind had gone blank.

'The OB. You wanted him brought in—or at least you asked specifically for top-flight specialists.'

'Of course. Sorry.' She shook her head, aware of her fatigue. Little points of light were percolating in and out of her field of vision. 'I'd forgotten his name. He seemed good on Friday.'

'He is. If you hadn't asked—'

'I know. It would have been a resident on call—who would have been very competent, I'm sure.' She laughed briefly. 'But this seemed one occasion on which my family's finances would actually be of some use to Heather.'

Now, why on earth had she said *that* to a near-stranger? The fact that she came from a quite revoltingly moneyed background wasn't something she normally revealed, even to close friends, until she had to. Not that Powell money was bad, per se...

Inappropriately, she found herself probing her own feelings on the subject more deeply than she had before. It was her adoptive parents' attitude to that money that she had a problem with—their arrogance about it, their ingrained certainty that it could buy them out of any of life's troubles.

Adopting Heather, knowing of her bad start in life, had been the one truly altruistic gesture of their lives, and it had backfired on them so badly that they'd been scared away from ever doing anything remotely selfless again.

'If only we'd adopted privately again, as we did with Jennifer!' Julia Powell had said once, at the height of the family's turmoil over Heather. 'It was a win-win situation. We got a baby with a decent background, and the mother got a nice financial bonus to help her finish college. With Heather, we let bleeding-heart attitudes sway us. . .'

Thus had Jennifer learned that she had been bought, as a baby, for an undisclosed sum from a nice, ambitious college girl who'd made a contraceptive mistake. It wasn't important any more. . .except that she had to wonder whether there was something more going on here than her simply wanting the best for Heather and her baby.

I guess I'm really looking forward to spending a good chunk of my trust fund on bringing up the grandchild Mom and Dad don't want, she mused silently. She managed to resist spilling *that* revelation to Dr Hartman, at least.

He had stopped by some strong shelves, and she realised they'd arrived at the maternity OR. 'You won't need to scrub, of course,' he said, 'but do put on all this, won't you? His gesture encompassed piles of gowns, caps, masks and shoe covers, and he was taking an item from each section himself as he spoke.

'You said you needed Dr Gilbert's permission. . .'

'I don't think he'll say no.

They entered the operating room together a minute later.

Afterwards, Teresa's birth was a blur in Jennifer's mind, the more explicit details mercifully glossed over, as they would be in the tale she would tell her niece one day.

They set off fireworks to celebrate your birth. I was

there. . .I couldn't wait to meet you. I loved you already, and when you came out you seemed so perfect to me. Tiny! But you cried and kicked like you were fighting.

Cried and kicked, that was, after those first moments of horrible silence when Teresa didn't breathe on her own and Will Hartman had to resuscitate her.

'Yes!' he said, when that first breath came. He made a fist of triumph and talked directly to the tiny child. 'Yes. I knew it wouldn't take much. You *want* this, don't you, little girl? You *want* your life!'

They set off fireworks. . .I had to say goodbye to your other mom then—your birth mum, my sister—so they took you away to the special baby nursery to look after you. . .

Dr Gilbert did a perfect job after Teresa had gone, stitching the incision carefully, with nothing in his attitude to indicate what everyone in the OR knew—that Heather would not survive. Jennifer thanked him for it, appreciating the sensitivity of the whole team during this time.

She didn't spend long on farewells, just said some quiet words. She hadn't planned anything and couldn't remember afterwards quite what had come out—didn't think it had been anything very profound or beautifully worded. Just, in essence, 'Goodbye. I love you. And I'll do everything I can for Teresa for the rest of her life, or mine.' Whichever is the shorter.

Your mum was so ready to love you, Teresa. She wanted me to be with you so I hurried along to the special nursery and there you were.

There, in that machine-dominated world where the common-sense fact that tiny babies like these needed peace and soft lighting and quiet voices warred constantly with the demands of the machines to be read, to be heard—numbers flashing on a screen, alarms going off, ventilators pumping, equipment trolleys bumping and rattling as they moved.

Jennifer had been in places like this before during her internship, but then she'd been on the side of the machines. She'd been the one who'd needed to interpret them, who'd followed up their readings with tests, reported the results of those tests and helped translate the numbers into minute-by-minute patient management.

Now she was on the side of the babies. Or one baby, to be exact. Teresa.

Will Hartman stood by her isolette, issued orders and worked over the baby with his team, rattling out a series of abbreviations and medical shorthand that would have glazed the eyes of anyone who hadn't heard it before. To Jennifer, though, everything he said had implications radiating from it like the ripples from a stone dropped in a pond. These first hours of life outside the womb were so critical, and so much could go wrong. Brain, eyes, heart, lungs. . .

She froze, overwhelmed, for long minutes as she watched. There had been so much to live through since Friday, and this was only the beginning.

Dr Hartman had seen her there. She knew it because she'd caught his dark glance, flicking in her direction. But he'd turned away at once and was ignoring her now, and if she hadn't been on the point of physical collapse she'd have yelled at him, Don't act as if I'm not even here! I'm this baby's guardian and care-giver now, and I'm a doctor. Don't try to use that jargon to screen what's going on with her!

But the words only drummed in incoherent fragments in her head, and stayed unspoken. She managed to move closer at last, walking as if in water, and arrived to lay weak, shaking fingers on the thick plastic cover of the isolette just as Will Hartman finally finished his work on the baby and his instructions to the nurse.

Teresa was almost part of the machinery now, it seemed. There were sensors on her chest and abdomen to detect temperature and oxygen concentration. There were ECG leads on her legs—tiny wires that would follow her heart rate and translate it into a series of spiky patterns on an oscilloscope screen. There was a moustache of white adhesive tape above her mouth to keep in place the ventilator tube that entered her nose and passed down her trachea. There was an umbilical artery catheter to enable the drawing of blood without the repeated use of needles. And on the thin skin of her scalp there were bandages holding her IV needle in position.

Jennifer knew about all this equipment, knew exactly how vital it was, but still she felt a terrible urge to simply thrust her hands through the two circular ports in the isolette and grab Teresa, pull off all those wires and haul her out, take her away, cradle her, keep her away from this monstrous technology.

Perhaps Will Hartman saw it coming. He stepped away from the isolette and took her arm, steering her gently out of the room and into a private space which she guessed was expressly for this purpose—to deal with the distraught families of tiny babies like Teresa.

'You know what it's all for. You know what can go wrong,' he said. 'That makes it worse, doesn't it?'

'Don't take me away like this! I want to see her, be with her.'

'And you will. But let's talk first, shall we?'

'No! What is there to talk about?'

Suddenly she hated him. Hated the fact that this was his

job—to torture babies, as it seemed to her tonight—and that evidently, therefore, he must *enjoy* it.

'You, for a start,' he answered. 'You flew here from Boston on Friday. What's your situation? Where are you staying? When do you have to be back?'

'I don't have to be back,' she answered, still hostile. 'I'm here from now on.'

'You must be staying *somewhere*, then.'

'In a motel Nearby. I'll go there to crash when I need a break—when Teresa doesn't need me here.'

'OK. Let's leave that for a moment. But "here from now on"? I thought you'd just started a paediatric residency in Boston.'

She shrugged. What business was it of his? 'Obviously, that's no longer practical. I'm sure they'll be able to shuffle things. I'd only been in the programme four days. There must be a waiting list. This can't have been the first time someone's dropped out.'

'And are you sure that's what you want to do? You've come a long way in your medical training to simply abandon what you've worked for.'

'I really don't need to hear this right now. . .' Tears clouded her voice.

He looked at her for a long moment, then said quietly, 'I'm sorry. It's just that. . . I've been there, that's all.'

'Been there?' She was still fighting him. 'You mean been through a paediatric residency? Obviously, if you're a neonatologist.'

'No,' he clarified. 'I mean, been at the sort of crossroads you're facing now, where the death of someone you love changes everything and you want to drop out of medicine altogether. That, effectively, is what you're doing, Jennifer.

It'll take a huge commitment to pick up again and restart your residency. I wonder if—'

'You wonder if I've got the commitment,' she finished for him, distracted by this issue so that she barely took in the rest of what he'd said. 'I don't care at the moment if I have or I haven't. And I certainly don't care what you think about it! All I know is that this is the only thing I can do.'

'Isn't there someone—?'

'No. There's no one else for Teresa. And don't tell me that if she. . .dies over the next few days or weeks or months then won't I have wasted my time because that is an *unthinkable* way of looking at it.'

'My God, I'm not going to tell you that!' he exploded. 'Hell, have you labelled me as this insensitive? We're going about this the wrong way around, I can see that. Why have I got you in here?'

Taking her arm again, he dragged her out of the tiny conference room and back to Teresa's isolette where the baby lay in a prone position with her head to one side, her thin red legs drawn up and her eyes protected from the NICU's bright lights by a white cloth.

'Look at her!' he commanded, his voice quiet enough to leave Teresa undisturbed but the authority very evident in his tone nonetheless. 'I'm sorry, this is what I should have said to you from the first. Look at her! She's breathing well. If she continues this way we'll start weaning her off the ventilator within the next few days. Her blood oxygen saturation started off a little low but it's climbing every minute. You can see it yourself on the monitor.

'You know about the use of artificial surfactant these days to coat the baby's lungs until she's mature enough to start producing her own. She weighs 720 grams, and her

Apgar score at five minutes was seven. Not a perfect ten, but at a gestational age of twenty-five weeks seven is extremely good. Dr Gilbert managed the delivery so that there was virtually no pressure on the head. We'll do an ultrasound scan at three days, but at this stage I'm confident we won't see any bleeding in the brain. This baby is doing very well indeed!'

'You have to have that outlook or you couldn't survive in neonatology,' she told him wearily, not ready to forgive him yet, and certainly not ready to show him the strength of her own will for this baby to survive.

'And *you* have to have that attitude,' he retorted, reading her emotions like one of the monitors that crowded around them. 'That's what you *have* to do for her—believe in her, believe in her strength and her health and her right, and communicate that belief to her. Here. . . Andrea?'

He looked around to find the nurse who would be working one on one with Teresa all night long. 'We're going to have Jennifer reach in and touch Teresa.'

'Let's have you do a good hand-wash, then,' Andrea Jones said, taking the request completely in her stride. She was a comfortably built woman of about forty, her jutting chest belied by a very sweet, cooing voice which immediately had Jennifer thinking, Teresa will like that. It will soothe her, not get her agitated and over-stressed.

She went to the sink that Andrea had shown her and scrubbed thoroughly up to the elbows, disoriented briefly by the familiarity of the action in what were otherwise such confrontingly unfamiliar circumstances. Then she came back to Teresa and reached in through the round ports of the isolette, aware that she was breathing fast and trembling a little. Such a tiny surface available to touch! One finger, moving a scant inch or so, could stroke Teresa from shoulder to elbow.

Mesmerised, she had forgotten Will Hartman and her anger at him, but he was there behind her, his voice low.

'You know how to do this,' he coached softly. 'No pressure, no friction. Just touch. And when you're touching don't talk. It's incredibly easy to overload a baby like this with too much input. Do one thing at a time, and as soon as there's the slightest sign of stress stop. You know the signs. Grimace, arched back, withdrawal of limbs, mottled skin. Those are perhaps the most common and the easiest to spot. Watch her, tune in to her.'

'I want to say something to her.' Jennifer turned away from the isolette and whispered the words.

'That's fine,' Will Hartman nodded. 'Stop touching, then, and lay your hands gently down next to her.'

'OK. . .I mean, she's not going to hear. She's asleep now after all that activity around her before. She's not even twitching in her sleep, but. . .'

'Who knows?' he said. 'I believe they *do* hear, at some level, even in sleep. Or do *know* anyway, when they're getting a message of love.'

A message of love. It sounded right so she said it, softly, her lips almost touching the transparent plastic. 'I love you, Teresa. I love you, OK?'

And then her cheeks were wet and she was crying silently, without even having realised she'd been on the verge of tears. Tears of happiness they were, as well as tears of total exhaustion, because here was a little human being, Heather's legacy, and she was *not* going to die, and she was loved.

There was silence and stillness from both Will Hartman and Andrea Jones while Jennifer just went on crying without sound. She was so debilitated that there was a part of her which had simply *detached*, it seemed, and could look at this scene and think, They don't know what to do. They're waiting for me to stop. I *should* stop. . .I *can't* stop. . .

Perhaps Dr Hartman realised the fact. He began to coach her again in that same low, cautious, gentle voice. 'That's enough now, I think. Just lift your hands and slide them out of the ports. We have nursery shut-down in about fifteen minutes, and I like to have as few people as possible in the unit at that time, so. . .'

'Shut-down?' The tears were still running down her cheeks, but dimly she realised that the routine and the terminology of this place was going to be crucial to her— possibly for months.

'For the babies,' he clarified. 'We turn the lights low, do our utmost to restrict the noise and movement and hold off on any invasive testing or treatment unless we have no choice. We do it for one hour on each of the day shifts, and in a one-hour block and another two-hour block over-night. It helps the babies to stay free from stress and starts to school them in wake and sleep patterns.'

'OK.' She nodded, trying to commit the details to memory. 'And this will be the—?'

'One o'clock shut-down.'

One o'clock? Could it be that late? Evidently. Still coming to grips with the reality of time, she allowed Dr Hartman to lead her away from Teresa's isolette, while Andrea Jones stepped in to check everything once more.

'Her O_2 sat is up to ninety-one and still climbing,' she murmured, using this common abbreviation to refer to the oxygen saturation of Teresa's blood.

Jennifer knew that ninety-two to ninety-seven was the desirable range. 'Almost there!'

'Yes, that's great,' Will Hartman said.

He reached for some tissues and she took a handful and pressed them to her face. I must be getting better, the detached part of her mind said, because I feel embarrassed now that he's seeing me like this. What a wreck I must be!

'Sorry,' she mumbled uselessly. 'Sorry about this.' She stuffed the rest of the tissues in her pocket and blinked. The skin around her eyes was burning with fatigue now.

'How are you getting to your motel?'

'I—'

'I'll drive you.' He turned to the nurse. 'Heading home, Andrea. I'll be in for rounds just before you go off if nothing more happens tonight.'

'You've hit the jackpot this weekend, haven't you?' she returned in that sweet, melodious voice.

He shrugged. 'It happens. Next weekend it's Jerry's turn.'

'And if he gets to sleep *and* play golf?'

'No, you see, Andrea,' he returned with smooth yet slightly teasing serenity, 'I believe there's a cosmic balance. At some point, I *will* make up that sleep, just as he's fated to miss a golf game eventually. I believe that, and it's faith that keeps this whole raft afloat, you know.'

'I know. . . Or at least, you've told me so often enough!'

Jennifer couldn't contribute to any of this. Couldn't. She tried to laugh a little at Dr Hartman's words, but her throat was rusted up. Or something. Tears. . .salt water. . . That rusts things, she thought vaguely. In winter, when they salt the streets to get rid of the snow, people's cars rust. The thought drifted off, escaped, and she couldn't work out whether it was relevant to anything or made any sense. There was a connection somewhere. . . Oh, yes. Driving. Dr Hartman had offered her a lift.

'I can get a taxi,' she blurted as she walked out of the unit, automatically attempting to match her stride with his.

'That's pointless. I'll drive you,' he insisted.

She didn't argue. They'd reached the elevator and he flicked a finger on the right button—an accurate, mechanical gesture which pointed to the fact that he probably spent as much time in this hospital, or perhaps more, as he did at home. There didn't seem to be anything to say so she didn't say it, and was too tired now even to think. Her impressions of their route to the parking lot were vague, too—just an awareness of carpeted lobbies and waiting areas, long corridors, signs for Radiology, Outpatients, Elevators.

In his car, which was maroon and new and nice, maybe a Buick or an Oldsmobile—something like that—they were both equally silent until, as he turned onto River Road, he asked, 'Which motel?'

'Oh, the. . .' She couldn't remember its name. 'The something Inn. It's down past. . . Well, under the highway bridge and then turn left, I know that. Opposite the parking lot of some big store.'

'You haven't even been there yet, have you? You haven't slept there at all!'

'Yes, I have! Of course I have!'

'Overnight?'

'Well, no, but I took a nap there yesterday afternoon, and showered and changed.'

'How are you going to manage for the next—? It could be months, Jennifer, you know that.'

She shrugged, on the defensive again. He was interfering. This wasn't his business!

'I'm having my car driven out from Boston,' she said. 'The motel's fine. It's a place to crash, that's all. There are

restaurants nearby where I can eat, and—' Dredging up
what the taxi-driver had told her on Friday afternoon, she
added, 'There's a pool.'

'You remembered to pack a swimsuit?' he drawled.

'I'll buy a new one,' she said through clenched teeth.

'Look, I'm only trying to help. You need more than just
a place to crash, don't you?'

'The motel's *fine*,' she insisted.

He'd found it, piercing together her hazy directions, and
pulled into its driveway. 'Room number?'

Of course she couldn't remember. 'Just let me out here.'

'No. It's one o'clock in the morning.'

'OK, then.' She scrabbled in her bag for the key and
read it off. 'One-four-three, along this side somewhere.'

He cruised slowly along until he found it, swung in to
the marked space in front, then switched off the engine and
turned to her. 'Get some rest. I don't want to see you again
until tomorrow afternoon. OK?'

'It's not your business to make pronouncements like that,
Dr Hartman.'

'Now, that's where you're wrong,' he countered with
calm confidence. 'It's very much my business. I'm Teresa's
doctor, and I believe in a family-centred approach to the
care of my patients. If you're determined to be her care-
giver—to adopt her—then you *can't* afford to gallop
headlong towards a breakdown, as you're doing right now.'

'You don't have much faith in my strength, do you?'

The sweep of his dark glance was an undisguised assessment. 'No, I don't. You're small and fine-boned, you're
coming out of your internship—the most gruelling year in
medicine—you're grieving and you're stubborn. On balance, no, I don't have much faith in your strength at all.'

She glared. 'Fortunately, your opinion doesn't have much influence over me.'

'I know.' If he was angry at her rejection of his assessment he didn't show it. 'Now, get inside and get to sleep, would you, please?'

'Did you think I was planning to do anything else?'

He didn't answer. Not in words, anyway. Instead, he lifted a hand from the wheel and brushed a tired strand of her black hair back behind her ear. She saw the gesture coming and wanted to duck it. She didn't need this man to touch her—to fix her hair, as if she were a child! But somehow she couldn't move, could only watch the movement of his hand, and when his fingers brushed her face they seemed to paint warmth there as palpably as if he'd been drizzling her with hot syrup.

She must have been holding her breath. Hadn't realised the fact, though, until now when it escaped in a sudden sigh. She felt close to tears again, too, torn between anger and gratitude. After all, he'd fought so brilliantly for Teresa's life in that first critical hour. She groped to find the necessary words. 'You—I—I'm grateful, Dr Hartman. This has been—If I've been—Thank you, I guess, is all I want to say. Thank you for Teresa.'

'Don't thank me yet.'

'But I—'

'Wait,' he insisted. 'Don't thank me yet.'

He waited until she had got her key in the lock then drove off, circling round the motel building to attain the street on her far side. She didn't go in straight away but, instead, stood and listened to the solitary sound of his car in the warm night air, lifting her face a little to find some freshness. The fireworks were long over, of course.

They set off fireworks the night you were born, Teresa.

The doctor who worked over you was so quick and sure that you were soon lying quietly. He just hadn't let there be time for anything to go wrong. I was mad at him, though. He wanted me to look after myself, stay away and rest and leave you to the nurse, but all I wanted was to be with you, so I made up my mind that I'd fight him if I had to. I was ready to do anything for you, Teresa.

Even if it meant making an enemy of William Hartman, she decided with ruthless determination. As she went into her room at last, she could still feel the warm brushstroke of his touch across her face.

CHAPTER TWO

ON THURSDAY morning Jennifer unpacked her suitcase. It had been sitting there for five days, nothing more than an irritant. Not even that sometimes. She simply didn't care that the ill-assorted jumble of necessities she'd brought with her was still in it, becoming increasingly tangled as she fished around each morning for something fresh to wear.

Now, though, three and a half days after Teresa's birth, something had changed.

Perhaps it was the fact that her car had arrived, driven by the nephew of Tom Dane, her parents' caretaker, and packed by the latter at her request with a second—and again rather ill-assorted—collection of things he thought she might need. Swimsuit. Hair-dryer. Medical textbooks. Teddy bear.

Teddy bear?

She looked askance at that one for a moment until she remembered. It had been Heather's. That brought on tears. Tom was a good man! He couldn't know that the moth-eaten and much-loved old thing would be far too much of a germ trap to be allowed in Teresa's isolette.

Or perhaps it was Heather's funeral that had changed things. It had been a private cremation, which had taken place yesterday. Mr and Mrs Powell could have made it from Hong Kong in time if they'd really wanted to. They hadn't, although Julia Powell had cried painfully over the phone on Monday.

'Jennifer, it's such a *waste*, such a bitter, bitter waste.'

27

And this time for once she didn't mean money.

'There's Teresa,' Jennifer offered.

'No, don't ask that of me! I can't go through it again, investing my love and never knowing if—I *can't*!'

'All right, Mom, but you'll understand if I do, won't you? I'm going to adopt her.'

Silence. Then Julia said hesitantly, 'I suppose it's useless to tell you—'

'Yes, it's useless to tell me.'

'You don't know what I was going to say.'

'It's useless to tell me, anyway. I know what I have to do, what I want to do.'

The conversation had ended shortly afterwards, an odd, poignant mixture of love expressed and hostility withheld.

Then had come a flurry of horrible, necessary arrangements—papers to sort out, Heather's few possessions to go through, her bills to pay, getting the formalities of the adoption under way.

Gloss over all that. Instead, focus on Teresa. They'd done her ultrasound scan yesterday, and it had come up clear. There had been no evidence of any bleeding in the brain, which was such utterly wonderful news that Jennifer had celebrated by complimenting Dr Hartman on his choice of tie. He had smiled and thanked her, then swept her with that sceptical, assessing glance of his and asked her if she's used the motel pool yet.

She hadn't. It was none of his business, and she told him so. If he was angry at her retort, though, he didn't let it show.

But there was something in his expression. He was biding his time. Like a crocodile, she thought rebelliously, hating him and wanting to lash out.

This phenomenon of wanting to lash out. . . It was normal

but not comfortable. It came quite often. An example...
Teresa wasn't yet on tube feeds. her intake of nutrition still
came purely through intravenous lines—fluids through the
line in her scalp and parenteral nutrition through a percutaneous line which snaked up a vein in her arm directly to
her heart.

Soon, though, if all went well she would be ready for
stomach feeds by tube, and that, as far as Jennifer was
concerned, meant breast-milk. And not just any breast-milk,
either, but milk from a mother who had delivered prematurely so that the composition of the milk would contain
the optimal proportions of fat, protein and a dozen other
components.

Riverbank Hospital, however, didn't have a breast-milk
donation programme. That was the first point at which
Jennifer wanted to lash out.

'Why not?' she demanded of Will Hartman. And why
hadn't she even thought about this issue before? What was
wrong with her medical training that she knew almost
nothing about breast-milk except that it was important, and
that it was difficult if a woman delivered prematurely?

He sighed and shrugged. 'The short answer? HIV. The
long answer—it could still be done if there was more commitment to screening donors but, with belts being tightened
all round, there isn't such a commitment.'

'Somebody should be something about it!' she had
threatened vaguely. 'It's important.'

'I agree. It is, and someone should. But everybody's
business is nobody's business.'

As he was then paged urgently to the delivery room, for
what was obviously an anticipated crisis, she couldn't with
any justification berate him any further.

She vaguely remembered having mentioned the subject

to Richard Gilbert on Sunday night, but hadn't heard from him. Then she had tried asking some of the mothers who were regular presences here in the NICU about donating milk privately, but the response had been off-putting. Two weren't breast-feeding at all, and two had been so evasive that it had come down to a refusal.

'It's *not* selfish of them, I know that,' she had sobbed to herself in the bathroom, pressing scratchy paper towelling against her reddened eyes. 'Their emotions are as stretched as mine, and yet. . .I *hate* them for it! If Teresa can't have the best. . .'

On Wednesday, though, Richard Gilbert had dropped in, while waiting for a delivery to see Teresa and find out how things were going. She had asked him about the breast-milk problem again, a little more able to focus on the issue and on his response. She'd told him the good news about the ultrasound scan, too, and he had promised to check in case there was a patient in his practice who might respond to a personal request from himself or his nurse to donate.

He had been so thoughtful about it, in fact, that her need to lash out had disappeared for a while, and she had come home to her motel late on Wednesday night and slept soundly for the first time since Friday, waking to the sight of her suitcase and all that stuff from her car.

Unpacking felt good—like an active statement about her faith in Teresa. I'm here, Teresa, for the next three months. . .which should be just the length of time it takes for you to grow enough to come home with me.

The motel room was pleasantly air-conditioned and fresh, with its permanent smoke-free designation, and there was room enough in the drawers and on the hangers and shelves for all her gear. In Boston she had been living in the modest apartment over her parents' three-car garage, which meant there were no problems now about having to move out of a place and she wasn't burdened here with anything she didn't need.

It was a spartan sort of life—a motel room and a few drawers full of clothes—but more than that would only have been a distraction.

When it had all been put away she almost celebrated with a swim in the pool. Almost. Somehow, though, by eleven she couldn't keep away from the hospital so she drove the short distance over, enjoying the cheerful fact that it was less humid today. The sky looked so gorgeously blue over the towering white brick and green glass that was the pile of hospital buildings, and thee was even a breeze blowing.

Her spirits soared wildly. Teresa's ultrasound scan was normal, her oxygen saturation was good—everything was good.

Except that when she got to the NICU it wasn't.

Dr Hartman must have been watching for her because he appeared at once, as if cutting off her approach, before she even reached Teresa's isolette. Looking past him, she could see a group of doctors gathered around it. Far too many doctors.

'Hi,' he said, and that was ominous, too, such a chirpy little word from such a very masculine and very professional man.

Jennifer reacted immediately, her scalp tightening like the hackles of a dog rising in suspicion. Her good spirits evaporated as if they'd never been. 'What is it?' she demanded. 'What's wrong?'

'Please don't be alarmed—'

'I *will* be alarmed! You know I will. Tell me what's wrong!'

He sighed. 'Well, her bilirubin levels are too high. You'll notice her jaundice.'

'OK. I was pretty much expecting that.' Jennifer conceded with heavy patience, 'as it's so common in premature babies. What exactly is the level? How will you treat it? Are you expecting it to worsen?' She fired off the questions rapidly and aggressively, and was angry at his careful laugh.

'Steady on! One at a time!'

All right, one at a time, but don't be so damned condescending about it!

She didn't say the words aloud, though she wanted to. Elevated bilirubin was nothing to get too upset about. It was common, it was well understood and it was easy to treat. Simply put, premature babies had livers which were not yet developed enough to process the yellowish-red pigment released by the breakdown of red blood cells, and they had lower levels of protein for this bilirubin to adhere to and thereby hitch a ride, as it were, to the liver.

The scary part was that while a certain level of this bilirubin build-up was harmless too high a level could cause a disease called kernicterus which led to permanent brain damage within five to seven days and, unfortunately, the danger point was hard to define. What was a harmless level in one baby could be a dangerous level in another.

'It's at level nine which, I'm sure you know, we'd regard as quite safe for a full-term or even a moderately premature baby,' Dr Hartman said.

'OK. . .'

'However, the level probably hasn't peaked yet so we'd like to start treating it now. We'll use phototherapy to start with.'

'Bili lights. . .' She used the less technical term.

'Yes.'

'And if that doesn't work?'

'It should. If it doesn't we'll look for an underlying cause. At this stage, there's no reason to suspect one, and I'm confident the light treatment will do the trick.'

'But a simple elevated bili level doesn't explain the large clutch of doctors, currently hanging over her,' Jennifer said, hearing the shaky note in her voice as well as the barely reined-in anger betrayed by her dark attempt at humour.

'You're right. It doesn't he conceded. 'She's started retaining fluid in her lungs and her exchange of gases is being impaired. We've had to turn up her oxygen and increase pressure in the ventilator at a point when we'd been hoping to wean her off it. Her heart rate has gone up, too. We're just about to do an ultrasound to look at her heart contour, and if we find it's as we suspect that means—'

'I know what it means,' she came in. 'Patent ductus arteriosus.'

It was a heart problem that was also extremely common in very premature babies. Immediately after birth, in a full-term baby, the blood vessel that had linked the pulmonary artery and the aorta *in utero* spontaneously closed, rerouting the blood through the now vitally important lungs. In premature babies this prompt and spontaneous closure sometimes failed to take place, causing blood to bypass the lungs and, after two or three days when the pulmonary blood vessel fully opened, creating a reverse flow from the aorta to the pulmonary artery.

'We have options, as you must know, too,' he pointed out.

'Yes,' she said heavily. 'Heart surgery. On a baby that's twelve and a half inches long.' It made those high bili levels seem about as serious as a splinter in a seven-year-old.

'No,' he answered impatiently. 'I'm not proposing surgery at this stage. I want to try drug therapy first.'

'OK,' she said cautiously, 'but that can have side-effects. Reduced clotting capacity in the blood, which could lead to—'

'Listen, remember how good her ultrasound scan looked? Remember how well she's been doing? *No* indication that she's vulnerable to bleeding in the brain. We'll try the drug and we'll monitor what happens and we'll make the right decision.'

'Said with all the arrogance of a doctor who thinks he's—'

'God? I don't, actually.'

'But you'd like to be,' she persisted, wanting to get under his skin.

'I wouldn't!' The hours are horrendous, the responsibility is agonising and the abuse is constant.'

'Why are you trying to make me laugh, you bas—' She choked on the word, but not with laughter, and suddenly he was gentle.

'Because I thought you might prefer that to crying. You've been doing a lot of that.'

That brushstroke of a warm touch came from his fingers again, feather-light beneath her eyes which were, she knew, ringed with the purple bruises of fatigue.

She shook him off. 'It helps. Worse if I don't cry.'

'True,' he admitted. 'I cried all through my internship.'

She smiled faintly. 'Everyone does. I think they make you if you don't do it on your own.' Though, in his case—despite what he'd just said—she had her doubts.

He glanced back over his shoulder to where Teresa's nurse on this shift, Helen Bradwell, was helping the specialists to set up their equipment. Jennifer liked Helen—liked the maternal roundness of her hips and the soft fullness of her blonde hair streaked with pale grey, liked her experience and her care.

'OK,' Will was saying. 'We're going to do the heart ultrasound, and then we'll be switching on her bili lights and starting her on the drug therapy straight away. Why don't you go—?'

'Back to my motel? No!'

'Just a thought. Don't—*please* don't—feel you have to stay here for the next twenty-four hours.'

'But I *do*, Dr Hartman! I do feel that. I do have to. For Heather, for Teresa and for me. Please let's not have this discussion *again*!'

He shrugged and withdrew into himself, up on to some elevated neonatologist's plane. 'It does seem to be a bit of a waste of time,' he murmured.

'Oh, *your* time!'

'Yes, my time—which is my residents' time, my nurses' time, the rest of the staff's time and ultimately the patients' time and that of their families.'

'Put very thoroughly in my place.'

The need to lash out was back again, and all she regretted was that her little sallies seemed so impotent. If she could have really *hurt* him she would have found it infinitely more satisfying. But he was taking it with the same steely good humour that a parent displayed when being flailed at by a two-year-old's tantrum-driven fists.

'Not put in your place, just—Oh, never mind!'

He turned from her and strode to join the crowd around Jennifer's isolette. Jennifer could only follow him, aware of several glances. It wasn't yet time for the afternoon nursery shut-down, and the lights were bright and the nurses busy over their babies. There had been a new admission just half an hour earlier, too, and Jerry Gaines, a confident, nattily dressed but slightly more junior attending neonatologist in the unit, was still working with flamboyant heroism over the tiny boy, with a nurse and a female resident hovering next to him.

A lot of mothers and some fathers were in today as well, and Jennifer wanted to yell at them, What's the matter? Haven't any of *you* faced down your baby's doctors or their nurses yet? You should. They need to be reminded—

Her inner diatribe died away. To be reminded of what? That this was *hard*? Realistically, she knew she was being unfair. There was nothing in Will Hartman's attitude that suggested he was ignorant about how hard this was. She tried to think back. What had he said on Sunday night about the death of someone he'd loved which had taken place during his residency?

At the same time she had let that revelation slide, and only now did she realise, He was really trying to tell me how much he understood. He was opening up in a way that most doctors wouldn't, and I never picked up on it. I should have done. I—*couldn't* but I should have. I wonder who it was that he lost. It must have been ten or eleven years ago. A parent?

It didn't seem likely that she'd ever find out now.

The ultrasound scan didn't take long and confirmed what Teresa's condition had indicated—the ductus arteriosus vessel in her heart had not closed.

Dr Hartman immediately issued orders for her drug therapy, and the infusion began ten minutes later through the percutaneous line. Jennifer skipped lunch, staying with the baby, and would have skipped dinner if Andrea Jones, who was on afternoons this week, hadn't deliberately wafted a bag of potato chips in front of her nose.

'You're going to stress Teresa out with the noise of

your stomach rumbling, Jennifer!' she sang.

She laughed unwillingly. Funny how much it hurt to laugh when you didn't want to, as if the sound was forcing itself through half a dozen constrictions in her chest and throat. She capitulated and went off to dinner, then came back and spent the night, uncomfortably and fitfully asleep, in a chair beside Teresa's isolette until the noise of the incoming staff and resumed activity roused her at the end of the four till six a.m. nursery shut-down.

Helen Bradwell was on, checking Teresa's monitors quietly.

'How is she?' Since when was her voice this creaky?

'Well, her O$_2$ sat's improved, and I'm going to try turning down her ventilator a little to see what happens. Do you think she looks pinker? I do!'

'Under these awful fluorescents? A bag of cotton candy would look washed out. OK, yes. . . Yes, you're right. She does look pinker,' Jennifer conceded tightly.

By the end of the day it was confirmed. The drug had done its work and the vessel had closed, sending Teresa's blood on its proper journey through the lungs where it gathered vital oxygen to carry through her body.

When Dr Hartman ordered the discontinuation of the drug's infusion late that afternoon and took the baby off the ventilator to put her on the less invasive continuous positive airway pressure—CPAP—instead, Jennifer experienced a giddy joy that had her feet light on the bland vinyl floor tiles of the unit and her heart singing. Even her voice. . . That horrible tightness was gone and she no longer wanted to ball up her fists and yell at people.

'It's like she's passed a test,' she told Will Hartman. 'And with flying colours. And to have that ventilator tube

out of her lungs, to know that her bili level is dropping. . .
Look at me, I'm shaking.'

'You're wiped.'

'I know,' she admitted.

'You were here—?'

'All right. Yes, I was here all night. Lecture me again.'

'I'm going to. Have you swum in the pool yet?'

'Not yet.' She felt happy enough to be cheeky, and added,
'But I will, if you'll join me.'

He laughed. 'You don't mean it, but I've caught you
now. I'm going to take you up on the offer.'

'No, I'm—'

'You said it, Dr Powell. Say goodbye to Teresa and let's
go. I'm finished for the day. I don't have a pool at my
place—'

'Oh, you do *have* a place?' she retorted. 'Rumour has it
that you actually live here.'

'I know, and at night I sneak down to a supply closet
and go to sleep on a pile of linen. No, I have a place but
it doesn't have a pool and it's hot and I'd love a swim.
Can I go home and get my suit and meet you there in half
an hour?'

'Why?'

'I just said, didn't I? Because it's hot.'

'Why, really?' she insisted.

'To make you take that swim.'

'*I'd* make you, Jennifer,' Andrea Jones offered—or was
it a threat? 'I'd love a swim! Only I'm on until eleven.
Look, if you don't agree I'm going to put it down on
Teresa's chart, you know. "Care-giver refuses to bathe.
Threatens baby olfactory sense threshold.' "

'Her what?'

Andrea grinned. 'So I'm making it up.'

'I do shower. I just haven't had a chance to—'

'*Swim*,' Will Hartman finished. 'But today you're going to. See, even Teresa is nodding.'

Well, that was stretching the facts. She was moving from a quiet sleep state to active sleep, which usually brought some movement, and this time she happened to twitch her head a little. Perhaps you could call it a nod.

It was enough, anyway. Jennifer capitulated. 'I'll wait for you in my room. Do you remember the number?'

'One-four-two.'

'One-four-three,' she corrected.

'That was a test, actually, to see if *you* knew it. So you really have been dropping in there occasionally?'

'Yes, I really have. I've even put away my clothes.'

'OK, I'll see you there. Half an hour?'

'Half an hour.'

When he arrived, as promised, she was in her costume, waiting for him. She was feeling a little frustrated because there had been a phone message from Dr Gilbert's practice nurse, Nicole Martin, at Riverbank Ob/Gyn, but when she had called back she'd only got the answering service. That meant that the office was closed for the weekend and she'd have to wait until Monday to find out if the call meant that a breast-milk donor for Teresa had been found.

The answering service could have paged the practice's on-call obstetrician for the weekend, of course, but since Teresa wasn't quite ready for stomach feeds it wasn't urgent enough to warrant that. The on-call OB probably wouldn't know anything about the matter, anyway, unless it was Dr Gilbert himself. So she shook off the frustration of this disappointment when Will Hartman's knock sounded at the door.

Today's a good enough day already, she reminded herself inwardly. Teresa's heart function is normal. I won't ask for miracles.

The swim was almost a miracle, though. She told Dr Hartman after ten minutes, somewhat hesitantly, 'I hadn't realised it would feel this good. Thank you for forcing the issue.'

He grinned. She hadn't realised he could grin like that, either. 'My motivation was entirely selfish,' he said. 'It *does* feel good.'

She watched as he stretched in the water, his body distorted into sinuous ripples by the lapping, aqua-green wavelets of the pool. Stripped of its professional trappings, it was a far more impressive body than she might have judged it to be in the unit.

There, the fluorescent lighting didn't do justice to the natural olive of his skin, and, of course, fashionable professional shirts and ties beneath a white coat couldn't begin to hint at the liberal dusting of dark hair on his chest or the well-proportioned contours of his muscles.

He wore navy swimshorts, generously proportioned— which she liked much better than over-revealing briefs, she decided. After all, she had no desire to be confronted too strongly by any evidence of his masculinity. He was Teresa's doctor and as such he was a vital person in her own life now, but he was nothing more.

And yet she realised, as soon as this emphatic thought had formed, that it was not true. He *was* something more. For some reason, he had set himself up to be her mentor, her guide through the emotional minefields of this experience. Otherwise, heat or no heat, he wouldn't be here now, swimming with her in this pool, and he wouldn't be saying quite matter-of-factly the words she had now tuned in to. 'After this, I'll take you home to dinner.'

For a moment she wanted to refuse, in the sort of polite yet categorical way that would let him know she meant it, but before she could form the right words she suddenly realised that she had changed her mind. If this *was* what he was offering—a haven, a sounding-board, a guard against burn-out—then she needed it.

No one else was offering it. There was no one else *to* offer it, and Will Hartman had been there from the beginning almost exactly a week ago—it seemed far longer— when he had come out to talk to her as she stood by the windows on the ICU floor, overlooking the highway.

'Dinner would be. . .' she began slowly.

'You need it,' he told her with authority. 'You need the break. You need. . .dare I say it. . .my wonderful home cooking.'

'I know. I do. That's why I'm going to accept, but. . .'

'But what?'

'No, no buts, I guess. Just thank you. I know what you're doing.'

'What am I doing?'

'Looking after me. And you're right. I need it. I like it, and thank you for being prepared to do it. It's. . .it's a professional courtesy for you, I expect, because I'm a doctor.'

'A professional risk, you mean,' he corrected.

'No. Why?'

'Because if it's risky and ill-advised to get involved with a patient—and it *is*—then don't you think it's doubly risky to get involved with the relative of a patient?'

'Get involved?' she was alarmed. 'We're not talking about getting—'

'No, we're not,' he agreed calmly at once. 'If you mean

the way the word is often used these days. But it's an involvement all the same. I'm seeing you outside working hours. I'm starting to build a relationship with you that's *not* merely the necessary predicate to my overseeing Teresa's case. That's an involvement.'

'OK,' she conceded. 'But not—'

'But *not*,' he concurred, and used a vague, formless gesture to finish their shared thought.

Definitely *not*. It would be entirely and utterly the worst possible time of her life to embark on such a thing, worse even than all the other worst times of her life—like during four years of medical school and her internship year. She hadn't thought of him in those terms once this week. There simply hadn't been room in the brimming vessel of her emotions for the remotest awareness of that kind for anyone and certainly not for this man, Teresa's doctor.

So why was it that now, suddenly, when they were both quite sincerely agreeing that this was not what they were talking about she was thinking of it, and was aware of him and of herself in their elemental roles of male and female as she had not even begun to be aware before?

The pool, perhaps. The water was so good. Sheltered by the surrounding courtyard and partially covered by a glass roof, it was limpid and cool enough to be refreshing yet warm enough to maintain body temperature for as long as they both wanted to stay in. The touch, the wetness, the buoyancy of it seemed to be caressing her limbs into a relaxation she hadn't known in a week. Longer, really, as those first four days of her curtailed residency had been more than a little stressful as well.

And, of course, they were scarcely clothed. Her suit was as conservatively cut as his—a pink one-piece with classic curves and shaping in its slender straps above boning that cupped and lifted her small but very feminine breasts just a little, a leg-line that emphasised her fine-boned thighs and a back that scooped to just above her waist. But even a conservatively cut suit offered little disguise.

She was treading water as he was and they faced each other, too far away to touch but quite close enough to see and to be aware of each other's scrutiny. He was looking at her now, too, and all at once she couldn't meet his gaze frankly as she had done until now but had to look away, flicking her glance quickly to a spot to her left where a patch of bright sun danced on the water.

'Mmm!' she exclaimed, and grabbed some meaningless words out of the air. 'It's just so perfect, isn't it?'

'It's not bad at all from where I'm standing,' he agreed on a drawl, and it was probably her own fault that she couldn't quite take the words at face value.

She swam, needing the movement—wishing her style was a little more competent and fluid. It wouldn't look very convincing if she pretended she wanted to get in some laps. This wasn't that kind of a pool, anyway. It was a pool for lazing in, and he wasn't making any attempt to do anything else she saw as she reached the sunny end and turned to stretch her arms along the moulded lip of the pool's rim.

He had sunk back into the water to douse his dark head, and now he was rolling underwater and arrowing along the bottom with a comfortable breaststroke. He was heading her way and probably *wasn't* planning to ambush her with some splashy prank—he was an attending neonatologist, after all—but, just in case, she swiftly pulled herself out of the pool and dived back in over the top of his emerging head so that she was halfway to the other end again by the time he surfaced.

The flurry of movement dissipated any lingering aura of sexual tension. . .which was too strong an expression for what had just happened, anyway, and she had probably only imagined the whole thing.

She heard his laughter. 'You got away!'

'Aha! So you *were* planning something.'

He shrugged. 'I'm not going to admit to that now, am I?'

'Now I *really* don't trust you!'

Who knew where it would have led, except that a trio of young children and their travel-stained parents turned up with a long day in the car to wash off? The parents were good about keeping the exuberant splashers at the opposite end of the pool, but peace was at an end all the same. After ten more minutes Will suggested, 'Let's go, shall we?'

'I'd like a shower to wash off the chlorine.'

'In that case, I'll stay here for a bit longer. Come and get me when you're ready, and I'll shower at home.'

It was such a reasonable plan that it didn't occur to her until she was already out of the shower and wrapped in a towel that she didn't have a clue what to wear. Two minutes later it emerged that this would be less of a problem than she'd initially feared as there were very few options available.

She hadn't had the time or the inclination to find a laundromat yet so a week's worth of summer outfits lay, disqualified from consideration, in a plastic bag awaiting a wash.

The few long-sleeved garments she had packed were out of the question in this weather, and any of the dressier things that Tom Dane had thrown into a second suitcase on her behalf—and she had to wonder what on earth he'd been thinking about there to have included a beaded silk designer original that had been a Christmas present from her mother—were hopelessly crumpled.

This left the navy blue washable silk T-shirt and matching silk shorts which she hadn't yet worn to the hospital as she'd considered them too casual.

If Will Hartman considered them too casual, though, he didn't comment so perhaps her frantic attempts at accessorising to dress up the outfit had paid off. Low-heeled navy pumps, a silver bracelet and necklace—also thrown in by Tom Dane—some soft make-up—optimistic, this— to distract attention from the fatigue around her eyes and a creditable attempt at pushing her below-shoulder-length black hair into the Most Popular Style of 1995. OK, so she was a little behind the times, but she *had* finished her internship year.

Will had towelled off and pulled on a T-shirt himself by the time she returned to the pool enclosure and, as it seemed redundant to take two cars and she didn't know Columbus anyway, she acceded to his suggestion that they take the maroon Buick. . .if it was a Buick.

It wasn't until they were about to climb into the vehicle that he finally commented, 'You look nice, by the way, so fresh and cool.'

'Thanks.' Then something impelled her towards honesty. 'I'm glad you approve because everything else is in the wash. Or needs to be in the wash.'

'Do it at my place,' he offered at once.

'No. . .'

'Why not?'

'Because I can easily—'

'Sure, very easily,' he agreed smoothly, 'but you haven't yet, and I have a washing machine and a drier, sitting in my basement.'

He was already moving resolutely back to her motel-room door.

'OK, then,' she conceded.

It *would* be convenient, just this once. He had swung the heavy plastic bag of clothes into the trunk of his car a minute later so she was then free to sit back in the passenger seat and experience the pleasant and woefully unfamiliar sensation of surrendering control. . .

'I feel as if I've scarcely lifted my head to the horizon,' she told him as they crossed a bridge over a rather sluggish river and approached a leafy suburb full of attractive houses, 'or opened my eyes to my surroundings for. . .' she sighed '. . .months! But today, suddenly, I'm ready to see again, ready to let go a little.'

'I thought you might be.' He gave her a rather searching sidelong look and his serious face was softened suddenly, and to a surprising degree, by a smile. 'In that case,' he added lightly, 'what a good thing I'm here.'

'Yes, it is,' she agreed dutifully, and it was only in hindsight that his comment struck her as being something of a two-edged sword.

CHAPTER THREE

HOSPITALS were universally known to have infestations of the very worst sort of gossip. After only a week at Riverbank—and a nightmarish week, at that—Jennifer had already garnered the generally agreed-upon evaluation of Dr William Hartman.

He was a great doctor and an upright, admirable and popular man when you got beyond a necessary level of reserve. Not bad-looking, either, some people would have added.

But he didn't know the meaning of the phrase 'personal life' and if he, indeed, *had* a residence other than the doctors' on-call room at the hospital—some people were quite convinced he didn't—then this residence would have to be the kind of bachelor hell-hole in which mattress and a TV were the only furnishings and a can of soda pop and some mouldy pizza the only contents of the fridge.

Jennifer was prepared for this. She was prepared, too, for something a cut above. After all, he *had* mentioned a home-cooked meal. What she *wasn't* prepared for was the reality that Will Hartman lived in a gorgeous house which betrayed all the trappings of a very well-orchestrated personal life indeed.

In this secluded rear yard he grew roses and vegetables, including tomatoes which were fat though still green on several vines. In his living room he kept musical instruments scattered about like sleeping pets—instruments that she was too ashamed to admit she didn't even know the names of. Was that a dulcimer? Or a lute?

And in his kitchen. . .

'When you said a home-cooked meal—'

'You didn't realise that you'd be expected to cook it yourself?' he finished for her.

'No! I mean, no, this is nice. I'd hate to be sitting around watching you.' She was, under his direction, making a garlic mayonnaise. 'I mean, I thought the 'home-cooked' part might consist of putting spaghetti in a pot of boiling water.'

'So you'd begun to subscribe to the general theory at the hospital that I lived in my car—'

'Car, on-call room, office.'

'And single-handedly kept the local pizza joint in business.'

'That's one of the theories going round and, yes, there are doctors like that, after all.'

'Which makes my own protective camouflage that much more convincing.'

'So that's what it is. Camouflage.'

'Of course. If people think you don't have a personal life they stop asking questions about it, which means you can actually get on with your personal life in peace.'

'Most people don't have to go to those lengths to protect their peace.'

'Most people aren't neonatologists.'

'And most neonatologists aren't much like you, I suspect,' she theorised rather brazenly.

He sighed, and stopped stuffing artichokes. 'It's the specialty I've always been drawn to, but I did have doubts for a while. . .if you're interested in hearing this.'

'Oh, I am.'

'The territory we deal with is *so* emotional, you see.

Controversial, too. As a group, we don't have a good reputation. Far too concerned with preserving the mere fact of
life without regard to its quality. Insensitive to the needs
of families in crisis. Eagerly awaiting our promotions to
the role of God next time the position opens up. Or if we're
not those things, if we do care and are sensitive and possess
humility, then we're on the edge of burn-out and
breakdown.'

'I wanted to guard against both those extremes, yet I
wanted to do my job well. It became clear after a while
that that meant protecting my life outside the hospital and
consciously creating the kind of beauty and peace and perspective that can be missing in my work. Hence. . .'

He waved a hand to encompass the details she had
already observed.

She sipped the white wine he'd poured for her, intrigued
and impressed. It felt wonderful to be taken out of herself
and away from the hospital like this—to have something
else to be interested in. She asked eagerly, 'So do you
actually *play* the. . .the zither, or is it just for show?'

'The *what*?'

'The zither.'

He gave a frank bark of laughter. 'If you mean the
mandolin. . .'

'I'm not sure if I do or not,' she confessed.

'Well, I play all of them.'

'But there isn't a zither?' she clarified.

'No, there isn't a zither,' he confirmed gravely. 'There's
a mandolin, a lute, a dulcimer and a viol. I don't play any
of them particularly well, but as the group I play with is
also cheerfully amateur and at home there's no one to hear
me practise. . .'

'So the hospital go *that* right, at least. You're not married.'

'Yes, I'm not married,' he agreed, in a way that suggested there wasn't much further to travel down that conversational road.

Briefly, she wondered why. Inclination, presumably. Or personality type. By the end of her internship year she had concluded that there were three types in medicine, as far as relationships went. Those who were fiercely devoted to their early marriage despite the stresses of the profession, those who were quickly sabotaging their early marriages *because* of the stresses of the profession and those who simply didn't have the energy left to pursue the idea of a relationship at all so that they married late or they married never.

She fell quite clearly into the third group—now more than ever, she realised, with Teresa in her life. She wasn't frightened at the thought. She'd always been single-minded, not a person who liked distractions. Marriage would come one day when she had more time and more of the right emotional energy.

Distractions, though. . . Such as getting more interested in Will Hartman's circumstances and his conversation than in this garlic mayonnaise concoction.

'Here. . .' He'd finished stuffing the artichokes, and now took the half-finished mayonnaise from her, beating it deftly with a fork. 'Why don't you go into the garden and pick some flowers?'

'Oh. Really? Um, which ones?' It wouldn't do to confess that this was something she'd never done in her life. Adult life, she amended to herself, but gathering bunches of dandelions once as a child from a neighbour's unmown lawn didn't count.

'Well, the roses are out so those, and whatever you think would look nice with them. Take these pruning shears so you get a nice clean cut.'

He took them down from on top of the fridge and she wondered if that was their permanent home, kept nice and handy within reach.

It was absurd to be nervous about picking flowers, but she was so she took a large gulp of the wine then left it behind and braved the lush wilds of the garden to gather a dozen or more of the sweetly scented flowers, laying them in the cradle of newspaper he'd given her.

She studied some of the other flowers but didn't have a clue what they were and didn't dare to pick them in case somehow they weren't suitable and he laughed. The roses were confusing enough, with their thorns and their differing lengths of stem. She didn't know where to cut, and wielded the shears clumsily at first so that his 'nice clean cut' was nowhere to be seen.

Gradually, though, she warmed to the task. There was a breath of evening in the air now, a faint coolness which seemed to come from the garden itself. Various rather benign insects—again she couldn't identify them—drowsed about, making an ambient hum, and the scent of these flowers was glorious.

She had a revelation.

He's right. Dr Hartman is right. It's dangerous for a doctor to be too narrow and I have been, but I *won't* be any more because there's Teresa now. I have to be able to do things with her, know *how* to do them, like picking flowers and looking at bugs and singing nursery songs. My life has been too focused. . .

It hadn't been her own fault, by any means. A Powell childhood was regimented. You had your main thing, which you concentrated on—in her case the academic study which had led her, from an early age, to medicine. Then you had the 'second string to your bow'. This was considered important for the creation of a rounded personality but, as with your main focus, it had to be diligently pursued and in an organised fashion.

Jennifer's second string had been chosen for her at the age of five. It was ballet, and she had been chauffeured to her lessons religiously four times a week for twelve years, had been kept lavishly supplied with an array of pointe shoes and pink and white and black practice clothes and had been taken to every season of ballet performance that Boston could offer.

Her petite build had suited the art, her dark hair had spent most of its time scraped into a dancer's topknot and the discipline of the training had given her more stamina and tenacity than her appearance would suggest.

She had got quite good at ballet in the end, as well as very knowledgeable about it and fairly fond of it, but it meant she couldn't do much else and had never simply lazed around the house and garden as she'd understood most other children to do.

It was a lifestyle choice that her parents had made for her, and in a dizzying, exhilarating and quite frightening glimpse of the future she realised, I'll be making those sorts of choices for Teresa. It's. . .it's overwhelming. . . wonderful. . .such a responsibility.

With her heart turning over with love and fear, she went back inside—carrying her flowers gingerly—and told Will Hartman vaguely, 'I. . .er. . .stuck with the roses.'

He glanced at her harvest. 'So I see. Uh, you've cut all the stems different lengths.'

'Well, all the stems *were* different lengths. I mean, there were the single ones on the long stems, and the little clusters where the stems were very short. Should I have just picked one kind? How do you do it?'

'I don't,' he answered simply. 'I just leave them in the garden, but I thought. . .' He laughed. 'I thought it was a task you might have felt at home with. A female sort of task, and a female sort of taste, too, to have flowers in the house. I've just been racking my brains about what we could use as a vase.'

'It is a female task, I guess, but I haven't—'

'Sorry.' He was still laughing. 'My fault. I was making sexist assumptions.'

She had to laugh too. 'So did you find a solution to the vase problem?'

'Peanut-butter jar?'

'That'll probably be appropriate for any arrangement I can concoct.'

In the end, though, he produced a wide-bellied glass jug and they fussed ineptly over the arrangement together, laughing again. Once she pricked her finger on a thorn and twice their fingers touched. Oddly, the latter infringement remained longest in her awareness.

'It sort of works, don't you think?' he concluded finally, standing back to look at their small creative endeavour.

'Sort of,' she agreed.

'My housekeeping talent is pretty much limited to cooking.'

'Whereas my speciality is—Oh! The laundry!'

He frowned. 'Forgot completely. I'll duck down into the basement and put it on, shall I?'

'No, I will,' she returned firmly, 'if you'll show me the way, and tell me anything I need to know about the machine.'

'No, really, I think it's easiest if—'

'We were talking about housekeeping talents,' she interrupted, 'and mine is laundry. *I'll* do it.'

It was a very polite little tussle, but a tussle nonetheless. Knowing why *she* was being stubborn, Jennifer wondered about his agenda until he suddenly brought it all out into the open by saying, 'I know what's going on here. I'm embarrassed about the state of my basement, and you're embarrassed about—'

'The state of my underwear,' she finished for him. 'I promise I won't judge you badly because of your basement.'

'And I promise I won't even look at your underwear. How about we do it together?'

His basement wasn't bad at all. Neither was her underwear, for that matter, but she conceded inwardly that both did betray certain intimate details about personality that neither of them might yet feel comfortable enough to reveal.

She learned, for example, that he had once attempted to get fit through the use of an exercise bike, but if the dust that coated it now was any guide he hadn't done so for quite some time. She learned also that he liked boxes and hung on to them. There was the one his microwave had come in, and several cartons emblazoned with the name of an illustrious maker of fine china, all stacked in a large pile in one corner.

Conversely, if he'd got any sort of a look at her underwear as she carefully sorted the contents of her plastic bag into lights, darks and delicates he'd have seen that she favoured the comfort of quality cotton in pastel shades, softened by the frivolity of fine lace.

He wasn't looking, though. He was surreptitiously dusting off his exercise bike. She put underwear and a blouse or two into the machine, found the 'small load' setting and the 'warm wash' setting and announced, politely pretending not to see his action with the dusting rag, 'I'll do the lights first.'

Half an hour later *he* went so far as to let her downstairs by herself to put the darks in the wash on 'medium load' and the lights in the dryer on 'low,' and *she* went so far as to peg up a pair of hand-washed pantyhose on a cord line that stretched across above the two machines, which seemed like a small, mutual advance in their degree of trust with one another.

It was time to eat.

He refilled her wine glass as they sat at a cane and glass table in the dining room that overlooked the garden, and she was feeling too relaxed, contented and hungry to worry about the fact that the first glass of wine had slipped down so effortlessly.

'This all looks. . .' She waved, speechless, at the table, then tried again. 'I hadn't expected such a feast, either for the palate or for the eye.'

He had produced chilled cucumber soup from a container in the fridge, stuffed vine leaves from a can and little pastry triangles filled with spinach and cheese from the oven where they'd been cooking on an aluminium tray.

'The vine leaves and triangles aren't home-made,' he said, 'but there are limits. . .'

There was a salad, too, of red- and green-leafed lettuces, with yellow slivers of bell pepper and green slices of avocado, button mushrooms, radish and fresh alfalfa sprouts. He had put chunks of lamb and onion on skewers beneath the broiler, and they were beginning to sizzle as he told her, 'Eat slowly because the artichokes aren't ready yet either.'

'Eat slowly? How can I possibly?'

'Pace yourself with fine wine and elegant conversation.'

It was the fine wine that did her in. Their meal lasted the whole evening, it seemed, partly because she had to get up every half-hour to do more of her laundry but also because he orchestrated it that way, making her savour each course and then distracting her with talk that wasn't perhaps elegant but was definitely interesting.

She hadn't enjoyed an evening like this in so long... which he'd guessed, perhaps. Had he guessed how much she needed it after the week she'd just been through? He put on music and said, 'This is what a mandolin sounds like when it *is* played well.'

It sounded wonderful, and... Did he deliberately wait until her attention was elsewhere in order to top up her glass again? Not always. There was definitely an occasion or two when she reached for the bottle herself.

And why not? This was a celebration. Of Teresa's improved condition, of that revelation about the future and everything she and Teresa would share.

'Thank you,' she found herself saying as they began their steaming artichokes.

'For...?'

'Oh, don't make me spell it out! It's obvious, isn't it? For doing this for me. For seeing that I needed it and then being prepared to take the time. For—for caring about Teresa, most of all. For putting up with me when I've yelled at you this week.'

'Have you yelled?'

'Yes! a couple of times. Not as much as I wanted to, I guess.'

'Ah! You wanted to yell at me a lot?'

'Sometimes.' She laughed. 'Why did I tell you that?'

He shrugged and smiled, as if he knew the answer to

the question better than she did but wasn't going to tell her. There was something in his gaze, something about the way his dark lashes had descended in a thick screen...an awareness... No, surely not! She dismissed the absurd notion firmly, and then watched as he dipped an artichoke leaf in the garlic mayonnaise and slowly pulled it across his teeth to scrape away the soft flavoursome flesh.

She felt...*younger* than him—as she was—and it was a nice sort of feeling that he had ten years of seasoning, ten years of experience and knowledge, and was letting her lean on it. Lean on it. Suddenly, lazily and happily, she liked the idea of having something to lean on...or someone...and didn't mind the feeling that she was slightly out of her depth. Drowning in wine, perhaps. Drowning in that liquid scrutiny of his...

When they'd finished their artichokes ten minutes later the laundry demanded her attention again with the imperious buzz of the dryer which marked the end of its cycle.

'Go,' he said. 'I'll clear up.'

She put the last load—the delicates—into the dryer and folded the rest, and when she came back up he had coffee on and a plate of chocolate chip cookies set out on the low table in front of his nubby grey wool couch.

Now there was lute music playing...or that's what he told her. If he had said it was a zither she would have believed that just as easily. Few of the world's great ballets were orchestrated with the use of either zithers or lutes.

She sat down and began to listen as he poured the coffee and brought it in. Then he sat beside her and she said impulsively and somewhat woozily, 'I wish *you'd* play the lute for me.'

'Ah! Now I *know* you've had too much wine.'

She frowned. 'I haven't.' The frown deepened. 'Or maybe I have.'

'Trust me, you have—and it's my fault.' He put out an arm to hold her small shoulder, which made her realise that she was swaying a little. She couldn't seem to do anything about it, however.

'But, more than that,' she pressed on, wanting him to understand, 'I'm *tired*, Dr Hartman.'

'Will, Jennifer, please!'

'Of course. OK. Will.'

'I know you're tired. Isn't it what I've been telling you all week—why I've been pestering you to swim in the pool and at least make the acquaintance of your motel bed?'

'And at some level I'm grieving. Really grieving, even though I'd already done so much grieving for Heather years ago. But the grief is tempered because there's the miracle of Teresa, only it's. . . Like the laundry. . .'

She groped incoherently for the right way to put it. 'I noticed that the water doesn't mix properly when it goes into your machine. You put your hand in one side of the stream and it's cold, and you move your hand a bit to the left and you get burnt. My feelings are like that right now. Hot and cold. Not mixed to make one warm pool but separate jets of hot and cold, miserable anxiety and giddy, joyful—Oh, damn!'

Suddenly her head seemed too heavy to lift and his shoulder, inches away, too strong and soft to resist so down she clonked her head, saying, 'Damn! I can't explain anything. Sorry. . .' She realised what her head had done and said, 'Sorry!' again as she tried to lift it, but he laughed softly and reached his arm around her to keep it there.

'You're completely wiped. I'd better drive you. . .home.'

The last word came out very oddly, which was hardly

surprising as she'd given a little, cat-like mew and turned her head from his shoulder to his face at just that moment. Presenting him with her lips like this made it fairly difficult for him to do anything but kiss them, and perhaps that was why he did—softly, carefully, as if not quite sure that she wanted it, as if making sure, every step of the way, that she was all right.

She was! Oh, she was! The touch of his mouth was delicious, creamy, tangy, firm and totally arousing. She didn't need or want him to withdraw as he was beginning to do, his low laugh gentle. 'Jennifer. . .'

'Please, oh, please. It's all right. I want to.'

'I know. I know that. And, believe me, I—I—Hell!' he muttered finally, and now there was nothing careful about what he was doing at all.

His mouth was everywhere on her skin, hungry and commanding, and her response was total because she loved it—loved the feeling of being deliberately swept away like this and lifted to this heightened plane of awareness. She moaned as he swept her hair back from her face with his palms so that he could reach her temples and the lobes of her ears and kiss and nibble her there. She fought him as he tried to pull her down on top of him because *she* wanted to be the one underneath, to feel the urgent male weight of him pressing against her thighs and her breasts.

He wouldn't concede, though, and a moment later she found out that to be on top of him was just as wonderful because then his arms could wrap fully around her and she could tease him with the silkiness of her hair against his face before he captured her mouth impatiently once more.

It was amazing how *big* a kiss could be. How endless and complete, and so huge in her awareness that there was nothing else at all. Everything was part of it—his hands slipping against the evanescent silk of her blouse and running along her summer-bare thighs, his breathing and the sounds he made, so very male, like the distant growl of thunder.

Her head was swimming and her eyelids were weighed down with the dizzy delight of this. She had to close them. She had to stop kissing him in order to breathe and steady herself, then she had to rest her head against his chest in order to anchor herself to reality through the rhythmic beating of his heart.

'Hold onto me,' she whispered hazily. 'I'm falling off the couch.'

'No, you're not.'

'It feels that way. Kiss me again!' She searched hungrily for his mouth, still not able to keep her eyes open or focused and frustrated because somehow those lips weren't there where she wanted them any more.

'Jennifer, do you drink wine very often?'

'Not often. Not when I'm studying. Except I'm—' He was confusing her. She wasn't studying at the moment, for the first time in years. 'Don't talk to me,' she begged. 'Let me rest for a minute against you and gather myself.'

'Sure. Rest! Rest. . .'

She snuggled into his chest more deeply and he began to stroke her from her hair down across her back to her thighs, following the curves through the cool, slippery silk. . .making her purr as sleepily as a cat. . .making her feel so deliciously warm and complete, making her. . .

The thought refused to reach a completion.

Jennifer stretched and rolled in the bed, then reached out sleepily in search of the form of a man beside her. She wanted to feel him again—his breathing and the touch of his skin, his shape pressed against the sensitive softness of her breasts and stomach.

She wanted a man, but there wasn't one. Her fingers found only cool sheets and then, higher in the bed, a fat feather pillow. She groaned a disappointed protest. He *ought* to be there. He really ought to. . .

Who?

Her eyes flew open. Not Will Hartman! And why was she in bed? What bed? What *room?* Will's room? The pretty sheet twisted around her as she turned and sat up, horrified. She had *slept* with him?

Had she slept with him?

Hazily, her head pounding suddenly, she tried to piece it together. She had definitely wanted to sleep with him, or her body had, and her body had tortured her deliciously with images and dreams of it for hours. Dreams of him kissing her, holding her.

No, *that* was real. Which meant. . . Oh, Lord. . . Did I? Is this his room?

She blinked. It was a nice room, rather feminine with its floral-on-cream sheets, elegant brass and white enamel bed and pastel-toned botanical prints on the walls. Sparse, though, in the detail of its furnishings. A spare room, in fact, and it suddenly occurred to her that she was still dressed in the same silk T-shirt and shorts she'd been wearing last night.

Last night? Yes, it was definitely morning now. *Late* morning. The sun was coming brightly through the windows, though central air-conditioning kept the room pleasantly cool.

Back to her clothes, though. If she was still in them then it was possible that she could stop panicking. If they'd slept together these garments probably ought to have been littered in a tell-tale trail across the floor, instead of hugging her tingling, aware body as they now were.

A dim memory detached itself from a webbing of dream images—her head lolling and bouncing a little on Will's shoulder as he carried her, followed by her own expansive sigh and contented burrowing into the pillow as he laid her gently in bed.

So she hadn't slept with him, but he'd had to bring her to bed and she'd slept the entire night away, uninvited, at his house. Not as bad as she'd first feared, then, but bad enough.

There was a clock in here, she discovered now. It couldn't be right, though. Eleven. Couldn't be eleven.

She got out of bed, slightly later than her head, which seemed to be in the process of splitting into three pieces and bouncing painfully in three different directions at once.

A hangover. This was a new experience, and one that— it was immediately clear to her—she had no desire to ever repeat. Standing very, very still for a minute, she realised that things were quite silent. Where was Will? He couldn't have gone, surely?

But he had.

Padding her way downstairs to the kitchen in bare feet— as her shoes made entirely too much painful noise on the hardwood floors—she discovered that it really was eleven, and that there was a note on the clean counter-top, pinned down by a bottle of painkillers and a large glass.

'Take two,' the scrawled note read. 'Drink. Eat. Shower. Don't forget your laundry. And don't apologise.'

Over the course of the next hour she obeyed four out of the six commands, purely for the sake of her physical well-being, then slunk out of Will Harman's house with her clean, folded laundry back in its plastic bag, devoutly hoping that all his neighbours were out on Saturday errands, and took a taxi straight to her motel.

CHAPTER FOUR

'I SAID *don't* apologise.'

It was Monday morning, very early, and Will had arrived for rounds. Jennifer had beaten him by ten minutes. She was nervous and distracted as she entered the unit because she knew she would see him today after the safety of him being off duty all weekend, his workload covered by Attending Jerry Gaines, an intern or two and a couple of residents, all of whom were starting to look familiar to her now.

'Of course I have to apologise,' she told him.

She had insisted on doing it in private, too, so she could do it properly, which meant that here they were in the little conference room with the door shut. She knew everyone would assume it had something to do with Teresa.

'Don't, please,' he insisted, 'because that implies that I don't understand what you're going through and why it happened.'

'Do you, though?'

'Look, you were physically and emotionally exhausted on Friday night. You were—as you still are—being pulled in two different directions by grief and hope. You very badly needed a release. Drinking a little too much is probably not a bad way of precipitating that release, and the fact that you then slept it off for nearly twelve hours was undoubtedly therapeutic, too.'

'Even though you had to carry me to bed?'

'You don't weigh a huge amount,' he pointed out

drily, sweeping her petite figure with his gaze.

His dark regard reminded her of the other element of her behaviour that she was determined to apologise for. 'I forced myself on you, though, and—'

'Ah,' he cut in, a noncommittal, medical sort of 'ah' that made her blush and groan inwardly. 'Did you?'

'I *did*! It was totally unforgivable of me. Personally it was crude—'

'It was anything but crude!'

'And professionally—'

'If you're going to say that it was ill-advised. . .'

'Well, I might have found something stronger.'

'No, Jennifer, please! Did it escape your attention that I liked it, and that I initiated it just as much as you did? I'd have to agree, though, that it's inappropriate. It's just. . . not what either of us needs at the moment when Teresa is my patient and the focus of your concern.'

'Yes.' She nodded, lifting her small chin. 'I'm glad you see it that way.'

'Am I allowed to say, though, that had things been different—'

'No, you're *not* allowed to say that,' she cut in firmly, desperately fighting memory and awareness. 'Things are as they are, and that's hard enough for me to deal with at present, without tying myself into knots over hypothetical situations as well.'

'You're right, of course. It was a pretty pointless and facetious thing to say.' There was a hardness to the lines of his body now, which had not been there a moment ago.

'That's all right.'

Now he was holding something out to her. A key. 'Here.'

'What's this?'

'Opens the side door that leads to my basement.'

'Wh—?'

'Do your laundry there from now on. I'm never home during the day. You can come and go as you want. There's no sense in you sweating in some noisy laundromat.'

'Will, I—'

'Please don't be polite about it. I wouldn't be making the suggestion if I wasn't sincere in wanting you to take it up. Let me make your life a little easier in a way that's harmless for both of us.'

Having her clothes in his machine, as opposed to having her body in his arms which wasn't harmless at all. 'All right,' she conceded. 'I'll make it mornings when you have rounds and whatever.'

'Whenever you like. As I said, I'm never home during working hours.'

'Thanks, Will.'

'Were you in here much over the weekend?' His sudden change of subject came as a relief.

'Less than I have been, you'll be pleased to hear.' The humour was somewhat grim and accusing, but he only smiled.

'No overnights?'

'No overnights. I—I realised how close to the edge I was. . .' Very close, when I'm prepared to fall all over an attending neonatologist whom I barely know, and when my memory of the feel of his mouth is still throbbing all through me. 'And so I tried to build some downtime into my schedule. But she's doing beautifully, isn't she? She had her eyes open for what seemed like ages yesterday afternoon. Allie Briscoe put a toy in—one of those little brown and white plastic bears. She wasn't tracking it, but I'm sure she saw it.'

It had been mesmerising and heart-filling to watch

Teresa. She'd seen a tiny yawn, a grimace, and once the startle reflex that was already in place, which made her tiny red hands—the skin on them dry now, and flaking a little—splay like starfish as she flung her arms to the side. She had tired quickly, though, of course, and drifted into sleep again.

'Yes, she's doing beautifully.' It was almost an echo of her own words, but somehow it wasn't quite sincere and she realised he must need to get to rounds now. She had kept him in here long enough.

'So. . .' She edged towards the door, keeping a respectable distance from him, and he followed her cue at once so that they came out into the unit together just as one of the residents, Sarah Jamieson, entered through the main door.

Last week Jennifer hadn't been in a state to observe anything beyond the immediate confines of her own emotional world but now, knowing that she would be part of this place for some weeks more, she had started to try and sort out who was who. She was curious about Sarah, who had just embarked on a very similar residency programme to the one Jennifer herself had cut so dramatically short in Boston, and evidently the curiosity was reciprocated.

'Hi,' Sarah murmured, favouring Jennifer with rather a long stare.

She was a tall woman of Amazonian proportions and looks—statuesque and stunning, in other words, with a strongly moulded mouth and thick hair the colour of honey-cake.

'Hello,' Jennifer murmured back, unsure if this was the tentative forming of a bond or the preliminary skirmishing of enemies. Before she could reach a conclusion the other woman's attention had already switched to Will.

'Sorry I'm late, Dr Hartman.'

He tweaked one eyebrow upwards. 'Are you?'

'Yes. Well, a little.'

'Don't sweat over it,' he told her, and they were off together to where the other participants of the round were gathering by the section of the neonatal intensive care unit devoted to the healthiest babies—the 'growers', who had beaten or avoided complications and would be discharged as soon as they attained the right weight or the right rate of weight gain.

Jennifer went back to Teresa, who was in the opposite direction.

It was a distracting day somehow. She discovered that a wise decision to put an episode of unfortunate behaviour behind you, and a sensible discussion about that behaviour with the person concerned, didn't necessarily mean that the whole thing could be shrugged off.

She was very aware of Will Hartman as he came and went about the unit, aware of the way he moved, of the different timbres of his voice as he spoke to parents, nurses or visiting specialists and of his name being used frequently by almost everyone who came through.

He was here a lot. It was in the nature of the specialty and since, as everyone agreed, he seemed to push himself even harder than most he spent time here at work at the nurses' station where another attending, like Jerry Gaines, for example, might have retreated to more private office space or taken work home.

When he did finally disappear at about three she was relieved, but she found that he still wouldn't leave her thoughts, which made her jumpy and very impatient with herself. In an attempt to anchor her mind she got out the medical textbook she had brought from the motel, a very dry treatise containing the latest theories on the treatment of prematurity. She turned to the section on patent ductus arteriosus to get a more detailed perspective on what Teresa had been through last week, and was soon lost in the familiar task of coming to grips with this dense material.

When the interruption came—in the form of a tall, slim redhead, wearing a white nurse's uniform—she didn't welcome it at first, but the redhead turned out to be Richard Gilbert's OB practice nurse whom she dimly remembered from ten days ago, wanting to introduce her to a patient of Dr Gilbert's who had also delivered prematurely—just a few hours earlier.

All three of them were about the same age and, thanks to Nicole Martin's cheerful introduction, Jennifer and the mother, Kathy Solway, established a connection very quickly. . .to the point where Jennifer probably jumped in far too soon to make the request which was uppermost in her mind.

'I'm looking for a breast-milk donor, Kathy. That's why Nicole wanted us to meet, and wanted you to hear my sister's story. I'm sorry. . . There's nothing in it for you. But Teresa *must* live, must thrive. . . Can you understand? Please think about whether you might be able to do this for her!'

Kathy was silent for a long moment. 'I have no idea,' she said. 'I'm willing. How could I not be? But this is so new—who knows if I'll succeed at pumping?'

'Would you like to see her?' Jennifer asked eagerly. 'She's so tiny.' She smiled. 'She makes your little guy look like a football player. But she's a fighter! If some sort of. . . financial compensation. . .'

'No,' said Kathy firmly.

'I'm serious.'

'So am I. For a start, I doubt anyone could tell us

what breast-milk brings on the open market. . .'

For the first time there was shared laughter between all three women, as well as from NICU nurse, Judy Lawrence.

'As for Teresa,' Kathy went on, 'I'd love to see her.'

So it was arranged easily, especially when compared to those difficult reactions from several women last week, and it seemed like another great omen for Teresa's future.

Retuning to Teresa's isolette after walking Kathy back to her baby, Andrew, Jennifer was in time to hear the shrill electronic piping of an alarm. A few days ago it would have panicked her, but now she just watched calmly as Andrea Jones, equally calmly, reached in and flicked her finger on one tiny red heel a few times until Teresa breathed again.

'That's happened quite a few times this afternoon,' Jennifer observed to Andrea, arriving at the isolette and laying her hands absently on its plastic surface. 'Is the alarm getting a little touchy or is Teresa getting lazy?'

'Don't obsess over every little thing, Jennifer.'

'Oh, I wasn't, I—' She stopped, a little taken aback at Andrea's response and not quite knowing what to say.

She had meant the question very light-heartedly. She really wasn't too worried. Teresa's breathing was fine now. She could see the rapid, rhythmic movement of it. Teresa was still receiving continuous positive airway pressure. This was a tube in one nostril that forced air at a light pressure through the pharynx, vocal cords and trachea and into the lungs.

It was less invasive and drastic than the ventilator she had been on until last Friday, but wasn't as good as the next step up—an oxygen hood. After the oxygen hood would come the final goal—breathing room air with its twenty-one percent oxygen content, like most of the rest of humanity.

Being a premature baby involved a series of gradations, Jennifer was starting to feel, and Teresa had already made her first by coming off the ventilator. Second, if you counted the closing of her ductus arteriosus.

No, today she wasn't too worried so why was Andrea still talking about it in that cooing, reassuring voice of hers?

'It's natural to plot every hour of her progress, as if you're keeping a graph in your brain, and to then respond with your emotions on a roller-coaster—way up and way down—but don't, if you can help it. Try and keep on an even keel—a *positive* even keel, of course.'

'Oh, I am, Andrea. Really,' she assured the other woman. Evidently this was just a general pep talk that Andrea Jones probably gave to all the parents of 'her' babies.

'Good girl, honey.'

Is she talking to me or to Teresa? Jennifer wondered. 'I guess I'll head off and get some dinner,' she murmured uncertainly. The last three words were drowned by Teresa's alarm going off again.

'What are you doing with that chart?'

Jennifer nearly jumped out of her skin at the sound of the full-bodied female voice just behind her. It was Sarah Jamieson—the Amazonian resident, as she had begun to think of her.

'I was just about to take a look at the notes for the past couple of days,' she explained quickly.

It was Tuesday morning, and she was feeling a little out of touch. She had gone back to the motel on Monday night after dinner at a nearby Mexican restaurant, and the evening had still been so warm—almost soupy, really—that the pool had beckoned temptingly. Last Friday it had felt so wonderful to ease her body into that limpid water. Will had been right. She should do it often. . .

Only she'd discovered that the water had become a little dangerous. The cool relaxed feeling it had produced in her as she'd lazed and floated and kicked had been far too strongly linked in her mind and her sensory memory to Will himself—the sight of his limbs rippling beneath the water, the cool slip of his touch on her skin later that evening. . . And she'd been trying to forget all that.

She had stayed in the pool for longer than she'd intended, trying to work through her confusion on the issue and get rid of these awkward and impossible remnants of feeling. Staying in the water too long then meant that she'd been much later than planned in getting back to the hospital, where she had found Teresa sleeping peacefully and Will issuing desperate orders.

There was a tiny, unwanted baby, trying its hardest to die, and after one last fight to persuade it to live the team conceded defeat. 'Except that in cases like this,' Will said, 'when the mother hasn't been to see him once since he was born three weeks ago, and when it's clear he was born with a serious cocaine addiction, you have to think that defeat is the wrong word. This little guy just didn't *want* it.'

It had been difficult. Unsettling.

It had made Teresa's little life all the more precious, and it had given Jennifer a new perspective on Will that she didn't necessarily want—to see him dealing with the limits to his skill, to see him grappling with issues of right and wrong, intervention and acceptance. He was a complex man, and a courageous one.

The net result of all this—the pool, the cocaine baby, Will and, yes, Friday's kiss—meant that she had left again last night after only an hour and had got to bed by eleven for the first time since Teresa's birth. Now, the next morning, not as refreshed as she felt she should be, she was also feeling out of touch and had automatically reached for Teresa's chart as Helen Bradwell, her nurse on this shift, was at the nurses' station.

Sarah Jamieson, still in an extremely hostile tone, went on, 'That chart is confidential and off limits. You had no right even to touch it. Put it back where you got it from at once before I have to get you thrown out of the unit.'

It was such an unexpected and unnecessarily forceful attack that Jennifer did as she was told at once, and only began to react emotionally once the chart was back in its place.

Reacting emotionally was a mistake.

'How dare you attack me like that?' Her voice rose higher in pitch as she spoke, though for the sake of the babies she exercised an iron control and kept the volume down. 'I am this baby's guardian and I am a doctor,' she hissed. 'No one else has objected to me looking at her chart over the past few days. If you have a problem with it then I suggest you at least attempt to observe a degree of professional courtesy in the way you tackle the subject!'

'Oh, *please*!' Dr Jamieson's eyes blazed. They were bloodshot, Jennifer noticed. 'Do you think I have time to tiptoe around your over-sensitive feelings? The chart is off limits to you. I've made that clear, and the fact that you're a doctor is irrelevant. If anything, it makes it worse. We can't have this sort of interference and questioning of our approach—'

'*What* sort of interference? And *questioning*? I've questioned nothing I simply want to be as fully informed as possible, and surely it's my right to—'

'Is there a problem?'

Both women jumped at the sound of Will's quiet voice. Locked in their verbal battle, they hadn't heard or seen his approach through the busy unit.

Sarah answered first. 'I caught her looking through a patient's chart.'

Jennifer rounded on her. 'You didn't "catch" me. That implies that I was reading Teresa's chart covertly, which wasn't the case as I had no idea I wasn't supposed to see it. *Am* I not supposed to see it, Dr Hartman?' She turned back to him. 'Not just "a patient's" chart, as Dr Jamieson put it, but my own baby's?'

'You know she isn't, Dr Hartman,' Sarah muttered.

Will sighed and answered with evident reluctance. 'Technically, Sarah is right. . .'

'Technically?' both women queried at once, then Sarah added, 'You're saying there's a tacit bending of the rules in certain instances, which no one's bothered to inform me about?'

'Look—Sarah, are you post-call?'

'Of course I am. Why, did you think I always sport these attractive red eyes? I haven't slept for twenty-eight hours. But what does my being post-call have to do with it?'

'You're overreacting after a rough night,' he told her, his authority—as well as his understanding—unmistakable. Unwillingly, Jennifer was impressed once again. It would have been a lot easier for him to use his position as an attending to simply barge through this problem. Instead, he was working at it, trying to leave both of them satisfied instead of fuming.

'And so are you, Jennifer,' he was saying now. 'I don't want to make a big deal of it. Technically, you're not supposed to look at Teresa's chart, but as I'm sympathetic to your need to be as informed as possible let me go so far as to say that if I'm not around to see then I won't know if it's happening, will I?'

'Is that—?'

'That's all you're going to get. And as for you, Sarah, don't you have some test results to chase up and report back on?'

'Yes, which is why I don't have time to be particularly tactful about her reading the chart. And now if *I* can finally get a look at it. . .'

She snatched the offending stack of papers and made them snap with a high-pitched, whip-like sound as she leafed through them. Then she frowned and looked up at Will. 'You're not going to order a—?'

'Yes, I am.' He cut her off. 'And I'll be doing it myself, with Kyle or Barry assisting, so I won't need you.'

'Fine, Dr Hartman.' Sarah flicked an uneasy glance at Jennifer. 'Has she been—?'

'I'm going to talk to her now.'

Something was going on. Jennifer found herself glancing back and forth between the other two doctors, now feeling very uneasy and suspicious. Sarah strode away at last but Will remained, as if waiting for an expected onslaught from her.

It came.

'What is it, Will?' she demanded at once.

Nothing, Jennifer. Everything's fine.

That was what she wanted to hear. What she *expected* to hear, too, because surely Teresa had had her brush with danger now and was out of the woods?

'We're going to do a spinal tap.'

He can't have said that. I just imagined it. I don't want to hear that. But I *did* hear it.

'A spinal tap?' she echoed blankly as a chill washed over her. 'For meningitis?'

'Yes.'

'I didn't—You didn't—' Her tongue felt thick and clumsy in her mouth. This couldn't be happening. It wasn't fair. 'You didn't tell me you suspected anything,' she managed at last.

'We've had her on antibiotics since Monday morning,' he said.

'Since *yesterday*? But what was there to indicate?'

'Those increased spells of apnoea,' he reminded her. 'I was being cautious yesterday.'

'I didn't even notice.' Except that in hindsight, yes, that alarm had been going off, and Andrea Jones had reacted oddly to her pointing out the fact. 'Why wasn't *I told*?'

'You were preoccupied,and you were trying to catch up on rest. I should have told you, perhaps, but. . .to be honest. . .I was waiting for you to pick up on it—which I knew you soon would. In the meantime there seemed no cause to alarm you. Yesterday the indications were very slight. Today I'm a bit more concerned. Her vital signs are a little less stable. I'm going to change her antibiotic to one that will pass into the spinal fluid in case there is infection there. We'll take the tap and then we'll see. It's a cautious approach, but—'

'No, no, you're right. If you hang back on treatment until you're sure. . .'

'It's often too late,' he agreed.

'I'm angry, Will,' she said helplessly.

'That I didn't tell you?'

'Yes! That you thought I needed *protecting* from it. I don't. I'm much stronger than I look, you know.'

Tears came to belie this statement even as she made it.

Furious, she brushed them with the heel of her hand and succeeded only in smearing the wetness more noticeably across her cheeks. '*Much* stronger,' she repeated stubbornly, as the tears renewed themselves.

He didn't challenge her assertion—didn't say anything at all—just watched her quietly for a moment with those dark eyes aflame, then said, 'We'll be doing the spinal tap in about ten minutes. Don't watch.'

'Why not?'

'Because I don't need to feel you there, studying my every move.'

'Oh, so this is about *you*, now!' Her continuing awareness of him felt like a weakness and made her angrier. Her body shouldn't be drawn to his like this, as if the warmth of his skin had a magnetic power over her.

'No,' he corrected her gently. 'As always, it's about Teresa. Let me do my work in peace, to the best of my ability, for her sake. Go and grab a coffee, and when you come back it'll be done.'

She wondered if this compulsion to obey him was a strength or yet another weakness but she did as she was told, even to the point of ordering coffee at the hospital cafeteria and only realising at the first sip that she would have far preferred something cold and fizzy. Which made her feel that obeying him *must* be a weakness since it was preventing her from even being aware of her own desires.

She determined not to be so docile in the future, and gulped her coffee so that she could head back and perhaps be in time to observe the procedure after all.

She was too late. And Teresa's isolette was gone. She panicked blindly for about ten seconds until she caught sight of Helen Bradwell in one of the isolation cubicles. They'd moved her, that was all.

'Because of the probability of infection?' Jennifer asked the nurse a moment later.

'Yes. Dr Hartman felt it was best, even though we're not yet sure exactly what we're dealing with.'

'It makes me feel as if my baby's a leper,' she said on a shaky laugh.

'You wouldn't want the other babies put at risk.'

'No, of course not.'

'Nor would you want Teresa exposed to anything else that might be flying around the unit.'

'I know that, Helen. It's. . .it's not a logical response. How. . .did the tap go?'

'Nothing untoward. Of course we won't know the result for a day or two, but the fluid was clear.'

'That's a good sign.'

'It is.'

It didn't stop her from crying, though, when she sat down beside Teresa's isolette and thought about pneumonia and sepsis and meningitis.

Then, at a quarter past one, while Helen was away in the bathroom, Sarah Jamieson came back and pulled out Teresa's IV. It wasn't as deliberate as that, of course. In fact, it was a complete accident but it happened so fast. . .

At one minute the tall resident was striding past the isolation room, and the next she had come inside, picked up Teresa's chart, put it down with a frown and reached in to the baby. Seconds later she was swearing under her breath and Jennifer could see at a glance that the IV line, which had been taped to Teresa's leg, was at the wrong angle.

'Was she due to have it changed?' she asked carefully.

'No.'

No further explanation was forthcoming. Sarah was too

busy preparing to reinsert it. Jennifer couldn't help watching the familiar procedure, compelled somehow by Sarah
Jamieson's anger and impatience. Too much time was passing. Sarah couldn't find a vein. She swore and began again.
And again. Teresa was crying, awoken from sleep, and
shrank instinctively from the sharp probe of the needle, her
limbs tiny against Sarah's large hands.

Jennifer endured the sight and the sounds in an agony
of silence. Sarah's third attempt failed and Teresa's cries
were becoming more and more distressed.

'You're hurting her!' Jennifer burst out finally, unable
to bear it.

'I know that!'

'Why can't you get it in?'

'I don't know! Because she's got no veins. They're the
size of hairs! As far as I'm concerned, she should have a
Broviac catheter, anyway.'

'No!' Jennifer reacted instantly against the suggestion of
this device, which was surgically inserted into a neck vein
and carried with it an assumption that it would be weeks
more before Teresa was ready for oral feeds. It *wouldn't*
be weeks more! She'd be ready to start receiving Kathy
Solway's donated breast-milk within a few days.

Sarah was gearing up for her fourth attempt. She was
glaring angrily at Teresa and muttering, as if it was the
tiny baby she was angry at. The needle looked absurdly
thick and huge poised above Teresa's almost
transparent skin.

OK, *this* time. . .' Sarah muttered.

'No!' Jennifer burst out.

Sarah looked up with coldly exaggerated
patience. 'What?'

'I—I think you should try a different site. If you just go

on jabbing. . .' the word stuck in her throat '. . .in the same spot. . .'

'I am not "jabbing"!'

'I didn't mean—'

'This kid has *no veins*! She's a nightmare! My fingers are thicker than her thighs. I'll get it in eventually, and perhaps if you would *leave* I'd get it sooner rather than later.'

Jennifer took a deep breath, marshalling her patience. To make an enemy of this woman would be a mistake. For Teresa's sake. . .'Look, I'm sorry. I didn't mean to question—'

'Yes, you did,' Sarah interrupted. 'Here! You do it! You're a doctor, as you keep insisting. So do it. You've got tiny fingers, too. Perhaps it'll be easier for you.'

And perhaps it won't was the unspoken corollary, hanging in the air.

'No, I'm sorry, I shouldn't have—'

'Do it! You'd better because *I'm* not. I'm going to lunch.'

At first Jennifer thought Sarah was bluffing, but she wasn't. She had gone, with a solid stride and a black expression, leaving Teresa still without her IV and still visibly distressed, as if she had been aware of the nasty personal vibes around her as much as she'd been aware of the pain.

The unit was unusually quiet—it was the middle of the one o'clock nursery shut-down, Jennifer realised. Where was Helen? It seemed as if she'd been gone for half an hour, though in reality it was only a few minutes.

'If I wait Helen can put the IV back in. I know she'd be able to do it.

But then there would be questions and it would emerge that there had been a bit of a scene. I've already had one run-in with Sarah today—and in front of Will. I can't afford to earn the reputation of being difficult. Staff hate difficult parents. I can't afford to get shut out of what's going on with Teresa.

And Helen still wasn't in sight.

I'll do it. I've done it hundreds of times. Never on a baby *quite* this small, perhaps. Certainly never on a baby half this precious to her. Teresa was still crying, a thin mewling sound which would have been easy to ignore if you didn't care.

'I'm coming, Terri-girl,' Jennifer crooned. 'You *do* have veins, darling, and we'll find one.'

Gently she put her freshly washed and gloved hands through the ports of the isolette. Sarah hadn't been exaggerating about one thing—the size of Teresa's limbs. The other day Jennifer had seen a father slip off his gold wedding band and put it onto his tiny daughter's wrist like a bangle, where it fitted as if it were made for the purpose. Teresa was no bigger.

But if I work *with* her size. . . Her skin's so fine I can see right through. Here's a good vein in her left arm.

She touched the fragile blue tracing with the tip of her finger—it was no wider than the mark of a fine pen—and applied the lightest pressure to bring it to greater prominence. Then she steadied her hand with an enormous effort of will, angled the needle and slid it beneath the skin.

She had the vein!

Teresa tensed, grimaced and mewled again, but then lay still as the needle remained in place. Jennifer attached the tubing and began to tape it, taking immense care not to knock it out or move it painfully within the vein. She heard a click as the door of the isolation room opened, but couldn't look up until she'd finished this last piece of tape.

There! Now, had Sarah come back belatedly to finish the job?

No, it was Helen in the doorway, looking pale.

'Her IV came out,' Jennifer said simply.

Helen nodded as she took in the scene, but Jennifer resisted the urge to explain and to involve Sarah. The whole incident shouldn't have happened, but it had. If Helen wanted to make a fuss then so be it.

'You don't look well, Helen.' It wasn't an attempt to change the subject.

'I'm not,' the nurse agreed. 'That's why I was away so long. Bathroom. Funny tummy.'

'Should you go home?'

'No. I had Thai food last night and it was too spicy, that's all. My digestion always reacts this way. I should learn my lesson and not eat the stuff, but I like it so much! Top end of me does, anyway.'

They both laughed a little awkwardly, then Helen added casually, 'Did you put it back in?'

'Yes. Sarah had three tries and couldn't get it.'

'Where is she now?'

'She went to lunch.'

'You shouldn't have.'

'I know.'

'How did it come out in the first place?'

'Well, Sarah was—' She stopped. 'Actually, I don't know what she was doing.'

'Probably checking for tissuing of the infusion.' In tiny babies like Teresa, the IV fluids could sometimes leak from the vein and begin to pool into the surrounding tissue, at which point the site had to be changed.

'Anyway, it just came out. Happens, sometimes, doesn't it?'

'OK.' Helen nodded.

The subject was closed, and somehow Jennifer was sure that Helen wouldn't mention it either to Will Hartman or Sarah herself.

Teresa was sleeping again already, starting the long process of shuffling herself gradually over to the corner of her isolette. Most preemies did it, as if seeking the confinement they remembered from the womb.

Jennifer said, 'She hasn't had any breathing problems for a couple of hours. That alarm hasn't gone off once!'

'No,' Helen agreed. 'Her colour is improving, too, I think. Those antibiotics are starting to kick in.'

When the result of the spinal tap came in the next day it was negative. Will gave Jennifer the news late in the afternoon in the conference room, and then watched as she immediately dissolved into silent sobs of relief and released tension.

'Would it cheer you up if I tell you we're going to try gavage feeding as of tomorrow?' he said.

Jennifer looked up, too interested in this news to think about what she must look like, with tears racing each other down her cheeks. 'Already? I was expecting you'd wait a few more days. Till Monday, or something.'

'Do you want us to wait?'

'I—You're the expert.'

'You seem nervous about it, that's all.'

'I am, I guess,' she confessed. 'With tube feeds I can start worrying more about necrotising enterocolitis, just when I'd stopped worrying about meningitis, and the very thought of NEC. . .' She shuddered.

'That worries you particularly?'

'Somehow, yes, because if the bowel is destroyed where do you go? I saw it in surgery once. A *tiny* boy with all sorts of problems from the beginning, then NEC and there was just nothing left when they opened him up. Coils of black bowel. There was nothing to reattach once they'd taken it all out. He. . .couldn't live.'

'She's already on antibiotics, Jennifer, and we're far more alert to the possibility of NEC than we used to be, as well as more able to manage its consequences in all but the most severe cases, such as the one you saw.'

'I've seen too much, haven't I? she said. 'I have a nightmare scenario to call to mind for every possible complication.'

'Doctors and nurses always do. They make bad patients and even worse parents of patients. If I had my way, they'd be banned from the unit.'

'You don't mean that.'

'No, I don't mean it. But may I ban *you* from the unit for an hour or so?'

'You're not going to—' she began, alarmed.

'No, we're *not* about to perform some hideous procedure on Teresa that we don't want you to know about,' he answered patiently, 'but Helen tells me you skipped lunch.'

She shrugged guiltily. 'Helen's a spy!'

'A well-intentioned one. *Did* you miss lunch?'

'Yes. . .' she admitted.

'Let's go, then. . .'

CHAPTER FIVE

WILL took Jennifer to a bookstore with a café attached and they sat in air-conditioned comfort while she demolished a spinach and cheese croissant, a piece of lemon tart and a tall iced café latte under his strict scrutiny. He drank a tiny, bitter double espresso himself, and she said accusingly. 'You're either on call, or planning an all-night pizza and movie marathon.'

'The former. I'm due back at six.'

Another three quarters of an hour. So soon! She realised that she was disappointed. . .and that it must show in her face.

'You make me feel relaxed,' she accused him again, 'as if your being away from the unit means that nothing is allowed to go wrong.' She laughed. 'That doesn't make sense. . .'

'Not really,' he agreed calmly.

She glared at him. 'I guess it's a tribute to your dedication. Somehow I don't believe you'd be here if you thought that anything was about to go wrong there.'

'Sounds like a useful belief.'

'I don't believe it because it's useful. I believe it because I *believe* it.'

'Don't think about it, then, just go on believing it.'

'I might,' she threatened distantly, then laughed again. 'This is silly! Thanks for bringing me. Let's talk about something else.'

'Books?'

'Books! What are they? Thick things with graphs and tables and diagrams, instead of pictures, and too many long words in Latin?'

'No. Glossy things with huge pictures in gorgeous colour of delicious meals or fabulous gardens or far-away places. Or things with no pictures at all—but *certainly* no graphs, tables or diagrams—just intoxicating, evocative strings of words to take you into another world.'

'And which kind do you like best?'

'Depends.'

They talked about books for a while and she was on the point of telling him how nice it was—how good it was of him to do this and how good for her it was—when he said after the first moment of silence in a good fifteen minutes, 'Jennifer, if you decide that this is too hard for you there are other options, and no one would question your decision if you decided to take one of them.'

'Other options?' At first she didn't even follow him.

'Teresa,' he clarified. 'Adopting her out, or finding foster parents for her.'

'*What*?'

'Hear me out.'

'Certainly!'

'You seem to be very emotionally racked by all this.'

'Wouldn't you be?'

'Yes, which is why I'm suggesting that you consider other possibilities. I'd hate to see you having a breakdown over it, tearing yourself apart over any long-term problems Teresa may have and never regaining the physical and emotional strength you'll need to get through your residence some time in the future.'

'So you're telling me—?'

'That it wouldn't be wrong to opt for self-preservation,'

he finished. 'There's no blood tie between you and Teresa. There are dozens of stable, loving, financially secure adoptive parents out there, waiting to take newborns—even premature ones. It wouldn't be wrong of you to go that route.'

She was speechless for a good minute, appalled almost to the point of laughter by the contrast between what she had been feeling—that this man's company was so pleasant and so good for her and that he *understood*—and what he had been thinking—that it was his mission to coax her into some awful, unthinkable decision about Teresa. Coax her into giving Teresa up, basically,because he didn't think for one second that she was capable of holding herself together through this.

'You. . . You. . .' She couldn't get out a coherent word, and scrambled to her feet in search of fluency.

It came, which was perhaps a pity because she ended up saying some rather drastic things.

'You arrogant, judgemental, superficial man! Why are you saying this? Is it a speech you make to all your parents? Or have I been singled out for special treatment because, in your opinion, I'm unusually fragile? What's given you the impression that I'm close to a breakdown? Is it because I've cried a few times? Yelled at you more than once? Collapsed at your house? Because I *care* and actually spend time with Teresa? Or is it because I'm small and weak and female, while you're a big, strong arrogant oaf of a man who knows best about everything?

'My God, to think I was about to tell you that I thought you were good for me, that you tapped something in me— a capacity for self-healing—and helped me find my footing, and peace, amidst all this. Gee, was I ever way off base on *that* theory!'

A speech of this nature wasn't fully complete without a dramatic exit, and she made one—more of an exit than she'd intended, too, because her leather bag swung on its strap from her shoulder as she turned and knocked over the last mouthfuls of *café latte* in her tall glass, sending the liquid pooling across the table and dripping on to the floor.

In the best tradition of dramatic exits, however, she didn't stop to wipe it up but carried on across the carpeted floor past the shelves of books, invitingly displayed, and out past the bargain tables at the entrance—to be greeted by the day's humidity, slapping her in the face like a wet sock.

The air was so thick that she could hardly breathe and she found that she was shaking which, for some reason, struck her as funny. . .and very sad. Tears came again, and she laughed through them, muttering aloud, 'He's right. I *am* having a breakdown, but I'll have *ten* breakdowns before I give up Teresa!'

Flowers.

They were gorgeous, but entirely inadequate. In Will Hartman's hands, as he stood at the motel-room door the next afternoon, the pink, yellow, white and purple blooms immediately spoke of apology, but they didn't speak loudly enough.

He clearly realised the fact and burst into speech before she'd even had a chance to take the fragrant Cellophane-wrapped bundle out of his hands.

'I should never have suggested that you give up Teresa,' he began.

'No, you shouldn't,' she agreed. 'I don't have a vase by the way.'

'Thought of that.' He produced a white pottery jug,

wrapped in green tissue. 'If you're going to insist on living in a motel for the rest of the summer you need some form of decoration.'

'Oh, I'm living in a motel for the summer? I thought, according to you, that I was heading for an imminent break-down and would be lucky to last here a few more days,' she pointed out sweetly.

'Jennifer. . .'

Suddenly there was a magnetic tension in the air between them, a powerful pull of awareness that was only height-ened by this skirmishing. Defensively—defending herself against her own treacherous feelings more than against him—she folded her arms across her chest and tensed her shoulders.

'I'm not going to let you off lightly, Will.'

'I began to realise that when I saw you speeding away in that taxi yesterday—and you'd told the driver to burn rubber, too, if those tyremarks at the traffic lights on Henderson were anything to go by.'

She laughed briefly, took the flowers and the vase, then stressed again, 'I'm *not* giving up Teresa, and I'm not having a breakdown.'

He sighed. 'Believe it or not, I wasn't putting down your strength or ability yesterday. I was letting you know— *trying* to let you know but failing miserably, obviously— that I know how hard this all is.'

'Do you?'

'Yes, Jennifer,' he said quietly. 'Listen, put the flowers in the jug and let's go to dinner. I want to talk to you.'

'And if I don't want to talk to you?'

'I'm your baby's doctor.'

'*My* baby. Yes! Thank you! She *is* my baby, and she always will be!'

'So it's in your interests to want to talk to me.'

'Put like that, I suppose. . .'

She did as he suggested and filled the jug from her vanity basin while he leaned in the doorway, watching her, then she heaped the flowers in an informal arrangement that suited their varied colour. Next, turning to him, she said, 'Now, if you want me to change.'

'I don't.' He eyed her simple dress of ecru cotton. 'It's a casual sort of place. Corn chips and salsa and margaritas.'

'Mexican?'

'OK with you?'

'Fine. What you've got to say will be more important, I'm sure.'

They drove up the highway past the hospital in his air-conditioned car, looped off onto another highway, then took a side-street and arrived at a big, noisy restaurant made to look like a peeling-plastered and electrically suspect Mexican cantina. It had a large veranda section enclosed in glass, and they sat there beneath lazily spinning fans, eating the chips and drinking the margaritas he had promised before ordering poblano chili soup and a platter of mixed main dishes.

Funny. Here she was, eating with him, very conscious of his body across the table and its effect on her yet she still wasn't quite ready to forgive him for yesterday.

I'm not the type to hold grudges, am I? she wondered uncertainly. He says he's going to explain. I trust him enormously as Teresa's doctor. Isn't that the role he's in tonight?

Confusing! Unsettling in the way it reminded her of their other dinner at his place when she'd let go so drastically.

I have no time and no energy to start bringing some murky male-female thing into this. We've agreed that it's an impossible idea. Why am I still. . .?

Aware of him. Horribly so tonight. Perhaps it was her anger. It had stirred up depths. . . Her body simply wasn't *clever* enough at the moment to sort out all the strands of what she was feeling into their correct colours.

It wasn't Teresa's doctor who was sitting casually opposite her, wiping a corn chip through the fresh, spicy salsa and crunching it in his mouth. And the appeal she felt in her own body. . . The questions in her weren't questions she wanted to ask as Teresa's guardian, but as a woman.

Make me understand you! she wanted to demand. Make me like you and trust you again so that this warmth I want to feel is OK.

'Ten years ago,' he said suddenly, out of the noisy silence of crunching chips and nearby laughter, 'I'd just started my residency. It was summer, as it is now. This sticky Columbus summer. I was on hospital call and my fiancée had gone to spend the night with her parents in Akron. She never made it. She was within about five minutes of their place, using a side-street she'd taken safely for years, when a drunk driver who was coming the wrong way ploughed straight into her. She died, of course. Instantly, I was told.'

'Oh, Will!'

'I was devastated, of course. Worse, I was angry. *So* angry. I took weeks off work and almost didn't go back. There was an anti drunk-driving lobby group that had just been started. I was ready to devote myself to it twenty-four hours a day.'

'But that sounds good, Will.' She was a little confused. 'Groups like that need good people.'

'Not people as angry as I was,' he pointed out. 'I wanted a chance to face down convicted drunk drivers and actually. . . God knows.' He twisted his hands around his glass. 'Personally kill them, I think,' he suggested with a crooked smile.

'No. . .'

'For a while, yes. Not the right motivation. I ranted about it to my fiancée's parents for hours on end. They were angry too, amidst their grief, but they made me see it wasn't the way to go. I joined the lobby group—I still give money to it—but I didn't make it a full-time commitment, and I went back to my residency. Eventually the anger became manageable, and so did the loss.

It took a good six months, though, before medicine began to mean anything to me again. Then for a long time it meant far too much, and people were right when they thought I didn't have a life apart from it.'

'And you see a similarity between what happened to you and what I'm going through?'

'Yes. Don't you?'

She groped for understanding. 'A goal deflected by tragedy?'

'Partly.'

'Priorities shifted by emotion?'

'Definitely.'

'An unhealthy degree of obsession and focus?'

'Maybe. I think it's what you have to guard against.'

'It's different, though. Teresa need me with her, physically and emotionally. She's not just a cause, an abstract belief, no matter how right and how strongly felt. She's more than that, and even though you see the possibility of a breakdown because of my care for her I see it differently. She's holding me together, Will. She's giving far more than she's taking. At the moment we need each other equally. We're vital to each other, and I can't look beyond that to how I'll feel about medicine when her need is less acute.'

'I've seen you reading medical textbooks in the unit.'

'To learn about her.'

'And are you learning?'

'Yes, a lot. It's like an intensive course in prematurity and neonatal care.'

'That's interesting.'

Anticipating the direction of his thoughts, she said drily, 'It's *not* a way I'd recommend gaining clinical experience.'

'Neither would I.'

They smiled tentatively at each other, and she couldn't help noticing what it did to his face, emphasising its sensitivity and intelligence. . .and its tiredness. Those lines around his eyes that her fingers suddenly itched to smooth away. That little tuck at the corner of his lips that she wanted to explore with the tip of her tongue. Not the way to think.

He really was an extraordinary man, and some of it was explained now. He'd lost his fiancée ten years ago. It had to help, when a doctor knew about loss, if that doctor had even the glimmering of an imagination, and Will did. It was there in the dark complexity of his smile, and in the way his hand came across now to lightly brush the backs of her fingers. . .with the scratchy corner of a corn chip.

Talk about tender gestures! How on earth could it suddenly be so sensuous when he lifted the chip to his mouth and crunched it, then washed it down with a substantial sip of the margarita in its salt-rimmed glass?

'Wish our soup would come,' she muttered. 'This drink is going to my head *fast*!'

It did come, and then perversely she was sorry because it hurried their meal forward and brought its end into view.

'There's a thunderstorm coming,' he observed, and she followed his gesture to see the purple curtain of cloud that was sweeping towards them. They both heard the thunder and saw the lightning a moment later, and the spectacle of the descending storm provided conversation for the rest of the meal.

The rain, when it arrived, was thick, and they could see it chasing across the nearby highway in sheets, flooding gutters and spraying up in the wake of cars. It passed on just as they finished their plates of *burritos*, and when they emerged ten minutes later the evening was suddenly fresh and filled with a steaming, green-gold light. Every blade of grass glistened and everything smelled clean.

Some last tardy drops thudded onto Jennifer's hair and she laughed. 'Blessed stuff! The humidity in this town is hard to take!'

'Almost worth it, though, for this freshness,' he answered, and at that moment she had to agree.

They'd moved well beyond the subject of Will's fiancée and what he had told Jennifer about her over their meal, but she felt compelled to close the subject properly and told him quietly, 'Thanks for what you said.'

'About Amy?'

'That was her name?'

'Yes, didn't I say before?'

'No, actually, you didn't. Amy. It's nice.'

'As she was. Not painful to think of her now. More like an old friend who moved a long way away.'

'And yet you've never married.' Hell! You don't say things like that, Jennifer!

Don't answer, she begged him silently. Let it slide!

But he didn't let it slide. He laughed. 'Never? Am I that old? That it's "never" now, and too late for me?

I must admit I don't think of it that way.'

'I—Of course not. Forgive me, from any angle it was a dreadful thing to say.'

'Then we're even. Because yesterday I said some dreadful things to you.'

'Oh, I think I gave as good as I got.'

He was still laughing, his face glowing in that odd, beautiful light. She was mesmerised by it suddenly—by the sensitivity of the little tucks around his mouth, the square yet finely moulded strength of his jaw, those arrowing brows. Why were they both just standing here? They should be walking to his car. He should be taking her home.

Instead, though, he was saying, 'Jennifer. . .' He said it in a suffering kind of way, as if she was being a nuisance. He moved closer and took her in his arms, planting a kiss, a soft, slow, masculine kiss. . .on her *forehead*.

Not the place she wanted it at all, clamoured her treacherous body. Far too intimate, nonetheless, insisted her too-sensible mind.

She closed her eyes, swayed away from him and mouthed huskily, 'Take me home.'

'Home?'

'To my motel, I mean. Of course.'

'Of course,' he agreed huskily. 'What else could you possibly mean?'

'Unless I meant. . .'

'Nothing, Jennifer. We both meant nothing.' She could hear the effort in his voice. His control was threatening to slip as much as hers had. 'And I'm planning to take you home right now.'

He did.

*   *   *

Teresa was gaining weight steadily now, though still with
agonising slowness. Ten grams here, ten there and then an
apparent loss which cast Jennifer down until Helen or
Andrea or Allie pointed out kindly, 'She just peed and
pooped, honey. Don't take it too seriously.'

'She's so tiny! To think that a few millilitres of liquid
and a few grams of solid in a cloth makes it seem as if
she's losing weight!'

But when she could look beyond the detail of each
weighing and see the big picture it was clear. Within a
week Teresa would regain her birthweight.

On Monday she had started stomach feeding through a
nasogastric tube, taking the small but regular quantities of
breast-milk that Kathy Solway delivered each day when
she came to be with her own baby. At almost four pounds
Andrew Solway looked enormous to Jennifer now, and
he was learning to suck which stimulated Kathy's milk
production and made things much easier for her.

When they came to the unit these days Kathy's wide
blue eyes and her husband's cool grey ones contained that
expectant but still slightly nervous expression that belonged
to those fortunate parents whose babies were almost ready
to go home—the 'growers', they were usually called.

Andrew had had no complications since birth and Kathy
was both highly committed and very well informed.

'When he gets up over four pounds and has gained
steadily for three days, with no setbacks, they say I'll be
able to take him home,' she reported to Jennifer one day
when they were both drinking coffee from polystyrene cups
in a quiet corner of the unit during the after-lunch nursery
shut-down. 'I'm so happy. . .and so scared!'

'That's fabulous, Kathy, and you'll do fine,' Jennifer
said, then added carefully, hating herself, 'Does this

mean. . .? You may not want to go on providing the extra milk.' And I'll hate you for it because it's so hard not to be selfish over this. Teresa weighs only just about half what Andrew does and she could still get necrotising enterocolitis or retinopathy of prematurity or. . .

'I want to go on donating,' Kathy was saying slowly, 'but, to be honest, I am wondering about bringing it in. I'm so much looking forward to not seeing this hospital for a while.'

'Oh, heavens, if that's all it is!' She nearly cried with relief. 'I can come by each day and pick it up.'

'And I can give you the cooler because I won't be needing it now. We're only ten minutes from the hospital—over in Arlington.'

So that was sorted out and a week later Andrew Solway went home to his pale, pretty nursery and his important baby job of growing and learning to smile and kick.

Life goes on, Jennifer thought, as she added the task of picking up Kathy's milk for Teresa to her daily routine.

Life did go on. Richard Gilbert was engaged to his practice nurse, Nicole Martin, apparently, while rumour had it that tightly wound, ambitious Jerry Gaines and his wife were splitting up. And Helen Bradwell was plotting a career change.

'I'm getting out, I think,' she said, but was hazy at this stage about what she'd do next.

Teresa completed her course of antibiotics, reached and passed her birthweight and had her phototherapy treatment for jaundice discontinued. That was nice. No more 'bili light' with its state-of-the-art 'superblue' wavelength shining down on her at all hours of the day and night so that her eyes had to be covered with a cloth pad.

Life went on. Several babies were discharged. Several

new ones were admitted. One died of severe congenital malformations that could not have been treated in any way.

Sarah Jamieson was delegated by a short-tempered Jerry Gaines to talk to the grieving parents of the little girl, and she did it so badly that Jennifer—who overheard because Sarah hadn't had the sensitivity to take them to the conference room—was wincing and biting her lip.

'You wouldn't have wanted this baby to live,' came the confident assertion from Sarah. 'She was very damaged. I don't know what went wrong *in utero*. With this degree of deformity I'd have expected you to miscarry, and it's a pity you didn't. Just try to forget about it and go on with your lives.'

'Wh-where is she?' the numb mother said.

'Where?' Sarah looked around, as if she'd misplaced a box of tissues or something. Then she dismissed the problem. 'Oh, it's best if you don't see her. Really. Just put this behind you.'

She reached out and patted the mother on the shoulder, a perfunctory gesture that came straight from some sketchy lecture she'd obviously had on 'bereavement issues' during medical school. Then she produced a card. 'This is a counsellor you might like to talk to. Do call and make an appointment. They say she's good. And now, if you'll excuse me. . .'

She slipped adroitly past the parents—they were still standing by the empty isolette which had held their baby until an hour ago during her brief half-day of life—and came in Jennifer's direction, to catch her appalled stare.

'What?' she demanded impatiently. The parents had turned to leave now, still numb and silent.

'Do you think you could have managed that with any *less* sensitivity?' Jennifer burst out, knowing she should hold her tongue but unable to help herself.

'You mean you had the temerity to *listen*?' Sarah demanded.

'I could hardly help it since you didn't give them the option of privacy.'

'Look, they knew two months ago that there was going to be a major problem with the kid. They knew it probably wouldn't live. Did you *see* it? If you're suggesting they should mourn—'

'Of course they should mourn! They're mourning what might have been, not the reality. They're mourning the perfect little girl they'd have had if things had been just a little different. They're mourning the miracle they were hoping for that didn't happen. And they're mourning—'

'I've got blood-work to do, Jennifer. Is there any point to this display of your expertise on bereavement?'

Jennifer took a deep, controlled breath. 'No, I don't suppose there is a point to it, in your case.'

'What's that supposed to mean?'

'Nothing.'

'Obviously you think I did a poor job with the parents. I disagree. I'm a doctor, not a social worker. I can't spend hours trying to empathise my way into every parent's deepest feelings. And if you weren't so *obsessed* with Teresa, to the point where all you can do is sit in here with not enough to occupy yourself and pass judgement on the way I do a job that I very much doubt you'd have the stamina and sticking power to do yourself, I wouldn't have to deal with your interference.

'You have no role that qualifies you to judge me, OK? My God, I'll be glad when you finally ship her out of here! Now, if I don't get my bloods done we'll have a lot more going wrong than a couple of parents reacting badly to a

death that was the best thing that could have happened
to them!'

She strode to the far end of the unit to get the equipment
she needed, leaving Jennifer shaken and still angry even
as she acknowledged that there was a kernel of truth in
what Sarah had said. She *was* in an invidious position here,
with too much knowledge to be simply a visitor in the unit
but no official role—no right to criticise Sarah's approach.
If Will had been here. . .

I wouldn't have said anything to her, she realised,
because I'd have assumed he'd do it.

She looked around the unit. There was plenty of activity.
Nurses watched their monitors, changed their babies' nap-
pies, wrote up charts. Some parents looked lost. Other
people must have overheard what Sarah had said, both to
the bereaved parents and afterwards. Very studiously, no
one was reacting.

Better than I am at minding their own business, she
thought. Too many concerns of their own. I shouldn't have
spoken out.

Later, as she left for dinner, she saw that Sarah had
cornered a newly-arrived Will over by the untidy herd of
five or six isolettes which weren't currently in use and
caught some snatched, heated phrases from the
other woman.

'Off the unit, that's all.'

'Sarah. . .'

'It's a problem for me. You told us to bring our—'

And that was all she heard. It might have related to the
earlier incident, or it might not. She should learn her lesson,
in any case. It was Sarah's problem, not hers, and Will's
problem, too, since Sarah had chosen to involve him.

But definitely not hers.

CHAPTER SIX

'TERESA'S five weeks old now,' Jennifer said to Will, struggling to make it a mere statement—an observation, not an accusation.

She was tired, having spent the night here last night, and she no longer tried to pretend to herself that her scheduling of the nights she spent here was random. It wasn't. It was quite deliberately tied to Sarah Jamieson's on-call schedule. If Sarah was on Jennifer stayed because she quite simply didn't trust her—either her judgement or her commitment—and if that was being paranoid she didn't care.

Somehow, though, she didn't want Will to guess quite how badly she felt about Sarah because for some reason he seemed to think the woman was good. She was certainly good-*looking*. Surely there couldn't be a connection!

'That was a brilliant paper on cryotherapy for the treatment of premature eye problems, Sarah,' Jennifer had heard him say a day or two ago.

Sarah had blushed and tossed her honey-gold head like a shy horse. 'Well, I worked on it—'

'It showed. You came up with some statistics I hadn't seen and put them together to create an incredibly lucid picture.'

'It's an interesting area.'

Jennifer thought so, too, but as always her concern began with the personal—Teresa's eyes—and radiated out to the general—what was the outlook these days? Statistically, what were Teresa's chances of seeing normally? Of wearing glasses? Of needing surgery?

No doubt Sarah could tell her, but she didn't want to hear it from Sarah. She wanted to hear it from Will.

'At five weeks,' she went on carefully, 'shouldn't she be getting her first eye exam? I haven't even met the paediatric ophthalmologist yet.'

'You've seen him, I'm sure,' Will said. 'Rather slight and stooping. Quiet, but parents generally trust him. Dr Fitzgerald.'

'*Him*?'

If she was matching the right impression to Will's description then it didn't inspire confidence, yet Will was saying, 'He's extremely good. Very thorough.'

'When will I meet him then?'

'Well, you may not. Not formally at this stage. He has a very full load. He prefers to keep a degree of personal distance in order to focus on the clinical picture and, unless the exam shows something unexpected, he'll probably just have me pass on his findings to you.'

'I don't like that, Will,' she told him. 'I'd really like to meet him—to *be* there, actually, while he does the exam. And if there's surgery. . .'

'Let's not think as far as surgery,' Will soothed.

'But it's very possible, isn't it? Statistically?'

He shrugged and nodded cautiously. 'Over fifty per cent of babies born at Teresa's weight do have eye problems, yes. Of those about ten per cent will need surgery. About a one in twenty chance, in other words.'

'So, when's the exam? She's five weeks.'

'There was no point in scheduling the exam until I felt she was strong enough to handle the surgery, if that's shown to be necessary.'

'But surely now she *is* strong enough—'

'Yes, and so the exam has been scheduled for next week. Monday morning, I think.'

'You weren't going to tell me, were you?' she said accusingly, hating the fact that she could be angry with him and painfully attracted to him at the same time. Her emotional wires were just so crossed at the moment.

'I was,' he answered. 'Of course I was.'

'Then why hadn't you? If you knew—'

'Jennifer, it's not a conspiracy, OK? Were you in here overnight again?'

'That has nothing to do with it.'

'Well, you're tired. On edge, aren't you? I simply hadn't thought to tell you about the exam, that's all. And as for your being present—'

'I *want* to!'

'I know. I'll. . . Look, I'll make a bargain with you, OK? I'll approach Dr Fitzgerald about your being present during Teresa's exam if you'll come for lunch on Saturday and help me deal with my tomatoes. They're ripening like crazy and I need a kitchen assistant.'

He grinned, but she wasn't ready to be softened yet. 'This, of course,' she said crisply, 'is the sort of completely orthodox suggestion you make to all your parents.'

He refused to rise to the challenge. 'So, I'm a little creative in my approach to family well-being. Teresa needs you to make salsa and pasta sauce. She doesn't need you pulling all-nighters every few days.'

She does or Sarah Jamieson will do something dreadful I know it. But for some reason you seem incredibly tolerant of her so I won't mention it.

'I don't, of course, have the slightest idea how to make

salsa,' she said instead, 'and my pasta sauces generally come from a store-bought jar.'

'That's not a problem,' he assured her cheerfully. 'As befits your junior role, you'll be doing the scut-work while I mastermind the operation.'

'As long as you don't forget *your* side of this bargain.'

'I'll be seeing Dr Fitzgerald tomorrow afternoon.'

'Good.' She glared at him, but he seemed maddeningly unperturbed by her fighting spirit.

Tomorrow was Thursday. She was on tenterhooks all day, the sort of jumpiness that swamped her sometimes these days, pinning itself to an issue such as the state of Teresa's eyes without a huge relationship to logic. In the morning she forced herself to stay away from the hospital. Instead, she sat through a leisurely and indulgent breakfast of pancakes and sausages, grapefruit and coffee at a nearby restaurant, but didn't enjoy it nearly as much as one was supposed to enjoy indulgent breakfasts.

As she nursed her third refill of coffee she wrote to her parents about what was going on, struggling to strike the right balance in how she said it all. They had made a clear-cut and self-protective decision not to be interested, not to be involved, and merely by mentioning Teresa's name she was challenging that—but what else could she do? If she wrote at all she had to talk about what was happening in her life, and that was Teresa. If she *didn't* write then it would seem as if *she* was cutting Teresa off from the closest thing the tiny girl had to grandparents, which she refused to do.

So the letter was awkward—to clinical, too rambling— and any time she thought of anything even faintly emotional to say she censored it before it reached the page.

This meant that in the end there was nothing about the

silky feel of Teresa's little thatch of startlingly black hair, nothing about the darling, bleary-eyed little grimaces she made and nothing about her first sketchy smile, which Jennifer knew was only a reflex at this stage but which hinted, nonetheless, at how her face would light up two or three months from now when the first *real* smiles came. Even blind babies learned to smile.

'Have you talked to Dr Fitzgerald yet?' she asked Will in a thin, tense little voice that afternoon.

After breakfast she had done her weekly laundry at his place, resolutely refusing to relax there. She hadn't even sat down, but had gone for an aimless, airless walk around the streets near his house while she waited for the machine's cycle to end. It was August now, and temperatures were regularly in the nineties, so a walk in the middle of the day wasn't exactly refreshing.

'Yes,' he said, in answer to her question. 'We met just after lunch. The Howell baby doesn't need surgery, which is good. And you can relax. He's happy to have you there on Monday. Nine o'clock. I...er...did stretch the truth a little.'

'Oh? How?'

'I said paediatric ophthalmology was a field you were considering for yourself. So don't let me down, will you? Read up on it?'

'Sarah Jamieson's paper, perhaps?' she suggested drily, but he seemed to take the comment at face value.

'Yes, that's an excellent idea,' was the mild reply as his gaze flicked over her, making her too aware of her own body and of its instinctive response to his. 'I'm sure she'll have a copy of it on hand somewhere, if you ask.'

'That good, is it?'

He looked at her again, his arrowing brows raised. 'Yes.

It *is* that good. She's very bright.' If there was a 'but' in there it went unvoiced.

'I'll ask her about it, then,' Jennifer could only say, reflecting that it served her right for being bitchy.

Have I started getting this out of proportion just because she couldn't get Teresa's IV back in place that time, and didn't seem to care about causing her pain?

She asked Sarah about the paper as soon as their paths crossed again, which was only an hour or two later, appending immediately, 'It was Dr Hartman's idea.' That at once caused Sarah's initially hostile and sceptical look to fall away.

'Oh, it was?'

'Yes, he says it's very good and, with Teresa due for her first eye exam on Monday, I—I want to find out as much as possible about what Dr Fitzgerald is likely to find.'

'Well, I don't have it on me, but I can photocopy it for you tonight. You'll have it by tomorrow, which will give you the whole weekend to...uh...tackle it. It's forty pages, including footnotes.'

'I should be able to get through it, I think,' she replied mildly, thinking, Is this just me? Am I hearing offence where none is meant? I don't even *know* which, I guess, means Will is right when he hints that I'm still not staying away from this place enough. I can't keep things in proportion.

Deliberately, then, she did stay away on Friday night, even though Sarah was on call again, and was then so nervous about what she would find when she went in on Saturday morning—Teresa back on antibiotics, off in surgery or surrounded by frantic doctors—that her legs almost failed to carry her into the unit. The immediate reassuring sight of Nurse Sharon Kovalik, calmly changing

Teresa's nappy, seemed at first like a mirage.

It was one of the best mornings. There had been a good weight gain since yesterday, and she had the precious chance to lift Teresa onto the scales with her own hands before the tiny girl was carefully replaced in her isolette. She could tolerate a little more stimulation now so, after waiting a while until she settled again, Jennifer sang her a song, and was rewarded by the sight of muddy blue eyes opening and the tiny movement of Teresa's head as if she was searching for the source of the sweet if rather scratchy sound.

'I—I think she knows my voice,' Jennifer managed foggily, and Sharon smiled.

'She surely does!'

Jennifer drove to Will's at noon, feeling giddy with release. He met her at the door, wearing garden-stained khaki shorts, a white T-shirt and battered old running shoes with no socks.

'You dressed up, I see,' she drawled, and he laughed.

'Didn't you believe me about the tomatoes?'

'I do now!'

There was a bucket of them on the kitchen counter-top, and when she glanced out into the garden, she could see more of the fat red globes, pulling the green vines down the wooden stakes with their sheer weight.

'We'll eat first, shall we?' he suggested, and she wasn't surprised to find that tomatoes were on the menu, eaten in the simplest way possible as part of a sandwich with cottage cheese on crusty bread, accompanied by iced juice.

They were unbelievably sweet and flavoursome, sliced expertly by Will with a very dangerous-looking knife that pierced the firm skins with no squashing.

'It seems almost wasteful to make them into something else,' she observed.

'Take a couple with you, then.'

'Well, I really don't have the facilities to—'

'No, I guess you don't. That means you haven't had a home-cooked meal in five weeks, not even a sandwich.'

'One home-cooked meal,' she reminded him, 'when I came to your place before.'

'True. Inadequate, still. I'll have to have you over more often.'

She mumbled a reply, unsure whether to take the suggestion seriously—perhaps because it sounded so inviting. His house was cool and peaceful and worlds away from the hospital. When she was here with him like this and could forget that he was Teresa's doctor, a man she sometimes wanted to attack and threaten and yell at, she realised how much she liked him and how easily she could relax with him.

She watched as he tipped his head back and drained his juice with as much masculine relish as if it had been beer or caffeine-laden soda pop, then he said decisively, 'Let's get to it.'

They filled two more buckets with tomatoes, by which time Jennifer's own navy blue canvas shorts and pink T-shirt were stained, too, and her fingers were sticky and yellow-green.

'They feel awful, don't they, tomato plants?' he said cheerfully, then added, 'Look, you missed a couple way in back there.' That meant she had to wade through the tangled vines and reach down towards the cool earth, where she had seen quite distinctly, huge and very vile-looking striped and glistening slug not ten minutes earlier.

He's being fairly merciless, she thought absently as she

spotted yet another tomato and went after it with determination. Fortunately, the slug seemed to have gone.

It turned out, though, that Will hadn't even begun to be merciless yet. Back inside he put on some loud soul music and produced, of all things, a pair of surgical gloves. 'Wear these when you deseed the chilis, or you'll burn your hands.'

'Oh, I'm deseeding chilis?'

'Yes. Unless you'd rather cut up several pounds of onions.'

'Um. . .'

'Didn't think so. I'm going to do them outside so the fumes can escape.'

'Try holding a piece of bread in your mouth.'

'Ah! That old wives' tale! Doesn't work for me, I'm afraid.'

'Oh.' She felt a little deflated. 'My parents' cook used to swear by it.'

'Did she, indeed?' He cocked an eyebrow at her statement and she felt uncomfortable, even as she questioned this response in herself.

So he knew a little more detail about her background now. So what? Some people's parents had cooks. It didn't mean they were necessarily spoiled or out of touch.

'It's OK, Jennifer,' he drawled, as if he'd guessed a little of what she was thinking.

'Good. Um, how finely do you want the chilis chopped?' she asked briskly.

'Pretty fine,' he answered. 'Like. . . Let's see. . .'

'Nail parings?' she suggested.

'Nail parings. Perfect!'

It was all quite a process. They didn't make just cooked salsa to preserve in airtight jars. They made garlic, basil and tomato sauce for pasta. They made cold blended gazpa-cho soup. And they made fresh *pico de gallo* salsa, laden with chopped cilantro and lime juice.

She was increasingly aware of him as they worked—aware of the brush of his long arm as he reached past her to grab the vinegar, aware of his bare, strong legs as he went out to the garden to gather handfuls of bright green cilantro and pungent basil, aware of his musky male scent blended with the more clamorous odours of cooking food.

When he was behind her she listened for him, and when he was outside, chopping onions, she missed him and stopped the staccato chatter of her knife on the big hard-wood chopping board so she could watch him for a few moments, unobserved. He had his back to her, and she loved the way his dark hair curled on his neck. She loved the way he moved, too, energetic and cheerful, deft and quick. Except, she remembered, he knew how to move slowly and caressingly, too. . .

The work was exhausting, and when he had her picking more fresh basil from the garden and slicing tomatoes for home-made pizza at five in the evening she finally said, 'You're actually *trying* to reduce me to a limp rag, aren't you? there's nothing accidental or unthinking about this. You *want* me to be wiped out.'

He grinned. 'Doesn't it feel good, though? After the 'bili lights' and the medical smells in the unit, and the fatigue that comes from being there all day but not necessarily doing much that's very physical.'

'Good?' she squeaked indignantly. 'You're suggesting that this feels good? When my hands are going to smell of tomatoes for the rest of my life and we could open a res-taurant with what we've made?'

'But doesn't it?' he persisted.

She sighed and admitted the truth. 'Yes. I—I haven't thought about Teresa or the hospital for hours. There's something far harder about mental and emotional fatigue than the physical fatigue of doing this. And I'm starving for that pizza!'

'How adventurous are you in toppings?'

'Try me!'

'Tuna and capers and artichokes? Pesto and mushrooms and black olives? Spinach and feta? All on a base of tomato sauce or tomato slices, of course, with mozzarella cheese as well.'

'They all sound great!'

'Then I'll make all of them.'

'While I. . .?'

'Sit outside with a gin and tonic, taste-testing the *pico de gallo* and reading the *New York Times*.'

'It sounds like bliss.'

And it was. He came to join her when the pizzas were in the oven, and they were silent for a while until he said thoughtfully, 'There's a phenomenon I'm becoming aware of in relation to you, Jennifer.'

'Oh?' She looked up to find him examining her with a clinical detachment that wasn't entirely comfortable.

'At the hospital you're so tightly focused on Teresa, so tense and bound up in your hopes and fears for her. You irritate me profoundly and make me want to shake you out of it sometimes—drag you bodily from the place—'

'Which, actually, you've almost done,' she pointed out.

'True, and with a very angry conviction at times that it's only because it's what *you* need, and I'm doing you a favour that gives *me* no pleasure at all—until I do get you away, learn a little more about you each time and see what you're like when you start to relax, at which point I realise I'm not doing this for you at all, but for me.'

'For you? How?' For some reason her body heat had risen and her heart was hammering.

'Oh, the usual, Jennifer.' He paused. 'I'm starting to want you quite badly. Surely you're aware of it?'

'No. . . No, actually, I hadn't been, really,' she said, her voice catching a little. Immediately she was flushing darkly and could feel the sudden tightness in her breasts. 'Because I'm far too busy—' She stopped.

He finished for her in a lightly caressing voice. 'Wanting me?'

'Yes,' she admitted, then continued quickly, 'We've sort of discussed this, haven't we? That it's a very bad idea?'

'Yes, but in view of the persistence of what I'm feeling I wonder if I was wrong about that. Hell! I hate talking like this when I'm not touching you!'

He rose from the cane outdoor chair and came across to her, pulling her to her feet and wrapping his arms around her with very male authority. 'You feel good, Jennifer. So good!'

'So do you.'

It was incredibly easy to surrender to his touch. She wanted it and he was offering it so why not? She didn't have the will-power to fight it. The strength of physical feeling he aroused in her somehow absolved her of responsibility.

It was like having a massage after running a marathon. She'd *earned* this—earned it by spending weeks at Teresa's side, by reading all that stuff about prematurity, by battling Will last week for the right to watch Teresa's eye examination this coming Monday and by proving to him that she was further from complete collapse then he thought.

Yes, she'd *definitely* earned it!

He didn't kiss her at first. He just held her, his arms tight and motionless and his chin stroking her hair. She burrowed into him, seeking the scent that had been tantalising and torturing her all afternoon above the smell of tomatoes and herbs. It was wonderful to feel that she didn't have to fight him—that she could give in to this.

He felt so strong today, and his strength was something almost palpable that she felt she could absorb if only she stayed in his arms long enough. His very name was nourishing.

'Will. . .' She said it, more of a sigh than a word. 'Will. . .'

'Jennifer.'

Now he wanted her mouth. He bent his head, cupped her chin in the palm of his hand and lifting it hungrily. 'Yes,' he said, his breath making the space between their two mouths hot. 'Yes, this is what we need, isn't it? Everything else just falls away. I've been fighting it, but I'm not going to now. Not unless you want me to.'

'Oh, no. . .'

Time stood still. Nothing existed but this.

His kiss possessed a dozen different nuances in turn. It was confident, almost arrogant, cajoling, demanding, gentle,playful, hungry, lazy. . .and she soon became almost drunk with the emotions that swept her—the sense of surrender and exploration, the emotional replenishment, the physical release. If he had decided that it was all right then it was.

She knew a need to discover more about his body and gave in to it immediately. She spread her hands across his chest to squeeze the tight, square muscles, running her fingers down across the hard corrugation of his ribs and cupping his taut and compact male behind.

He groaned at what she was doing to him and she felt the vibration of the sound against her acutely sensitised breast. She arched convulsively so that his lips trailed to the fine, stretched skin of her neck.

He tried to recapture her mouth but she had brought her hands up now, to run them through his hair and then touch the bow of his lips with the sensitive pads of her fingers. She felt her strength ebbing and stepped back, and back again, until she sank against the side of the house and his hands came up to spread on either side of her, imprisoning her and forcing her—as if she wanted to do anything else— to accept his kiss again.

'Jennifer. . . You feel amazing in my arms. It's electric.'

'Yes. . .'

'I could make love to you now. . .'

'You can,' she promised hazily and rashly. There seemed no reason not to say it. She arched against him again, deliberately rubbing the tightly furled buds of her breasts against his T-shirt, making him groan and laugh.

'Apart from the little matter of the pizza cooking,' he said.

'We could. . .um. . .turn the oven off,' she mumbled, closing her eyes.

She didn't really want to see the daylight, the glimpse of another house over his back fence beyond the lush garden. She didn't want to think about the fact that the rest of the world was out there and was a far more complicated place than this moment she was lost in.

'That doesn't sound like a good idea,' he was saying.

'I'm not hungry,' she assured him desperately.

'You said you were starving before.'

'Mmm, yes, I did. I—' She blinked and opened her eyes again. 'I guess. . .' She felt very lost and vague. 'I guess this is bad timing. We should wait until after dinner.'

'That's a sensible suggestion,' came his mild response.

She focused on him more closely. Something had changed. His regard was far more detached now. Almost clinical.

'What's the matter, Will?' she said uncertainly.

He opened his mouth, then shook his head. 'Nothing.' He smiled and kissed her again, and she returned to his arms with relief, snuggling there like a child.

'That's OK, then,' she said happily.

'Mmm. But I'd better check the oven.'

'I'll come, too. I don't want to be by myself.'

He frowned at this. 'OK.'

So she followed him and they examined the sizzling pizza together. She'd have said they were done but he pronounced with authority that they needed another minute. She certainly wasn't prepared to argue the point as he clearly knew far more about making pizza than she did. He closed the oven door again and turned to the sink to start rinsing the chopping board and a couple of other dishes, then he braved the oven's fierce heat once more to pull out the three circular metal pizza plates with their bubbling contents.

'Just right!'

They were completely delicious—savoury and complex, with the juicy sweetness of the tomatoes to counteract, the saltiness of tuna and olives and feta cheese. He offered her white wine, as he'd done last time she ate here, but she frowned and said uncertainly, 'Perhaps I'd better not.'

He gravely commended her for her good sense and this struck her as suspicious, although the twinkle in his dark eyes and the softness of a tiny smile around his mouth

sweetened the words—the way his tomatoes had sweetened
the pizza.

She had expected him to hurry through the meal and
then suggestively propose bed before the last mouthful was
fully swallowed but he didn't, stretching dinner with
seconds and salad and cake and coffee and *watching* her
all the while in that way she was beginning to distrust
quite a bit.

Finally, confused and acting from the simplicity of the
sensuous release she'd discovered in his arms before dinner,
she stretched and got up from the couch where she'd been
sitting and came over to him—he was sprawled on the
bigger couch—and slid beside him to say with an awkward
mixture of uncertainty and kittenish sensuality, 'Will?
Please kiss me again!'

'No,' he answered tenderly. 'I'm going to send you
home, sweetheart.'

'Why? I thought you wanted it.'

Since she hadn't drunk anything stronger than coffee she
had no excuse for this petulant frankness, but somehow
she was at sea and didn't know how else to phrase it.

'I do want it,' he answered.

'And so do I so—'

He sighed. 'It's not enough, Jennifer.'

'But—'

'Let's not pull it all apart. You'll argue—'

'Of course I will!'

'So I'll just say not tonight. Wait. Take another look at
what you're feeling.'

'What I'm feeling right now is embarrassed!' she
retorted. 'You led me—'

'Yes,' he cut in. 'I led you, and you followed like a
little lamb.'

'I don't generally think of myself as a lamb, actually! To the slaughter, did you mean?'

'No, that's a bit strong.'

'I should think so!'

'But on the right track.'

'You—You arrogant—!'

'Don't, Jennifer,' he begged rather tiredly. 'Don't turn it into a fight. It's not one, as far as I'm concerned.'

'So you do intend to sleep with me at some point,' she replied drily. 'At a point where *you* deem it appropriate.'

'No, at a time when *you* are capable of making a more balanced decision about whether it's what you really want, Jennifer,' he said quietly, as if her badgering had finally defeated him. 'Tonight I'd have been taking advantage of you—so much so that even now you don't believe me. Let's leave it, OK? Take things one day at a time.'

'Right. Sure. . .'

What else could she say?

Inevitably, it made for an awkward end to the evening. He was trying to be nice and he would have succeeded if she'd let him, but instead she was too unsure exactly what that had all been about.

He seemed to be questioning her ability to understand her own feelings, and perhaps he was right because she was certainly confused now—angry, disappointed, embarrassed, yearning, wanting him still but dimly knowing that if she'd woken up tomorrow morning in his bed she'd have felt overwhelmed by the addition of yet another strand of feeling in what was already a chronic condition of dangerous emotional overload.

'I guess I'd better go, then,' she said finally.

'It is after ten.'

'She didn't believe it at first but he was right, of course. It was ten-fifteen.

'Going to the hospital tonight?' he asked.

'I—No. I hadn't planned to.'

'She'll keep till tomorrow,' he agreed.

Back at the motel, though, she couldn't sleep. She picked up the forty-page paper on retinopathy of prematurity which Sarah Jamieson had left for her in the unit that morning and began to study it, sitting up in bed in her cotton pyjamas. The combination of cold statistics and clinical descriptions of detached retinas and irreversible blindness then frightened her so much that she dressed again and drove to the hospital, arriving at two in the morning to find Allie Briscoe, who was doing the night shift tonight, almost asleep beside Teresa's isolette.

She stayed until dawn, watching the sleeping baby for a long time. She helped to set up her four o'clock feed, then finally dozed off herself in the chair just a few feet from the baby so that she felt wretched and stiff by the time she left again and didn't know what she had accomplished by being there. Worrying about the possibility of blindness, she hadn't exactly been flooding Teresa with positive vibes.

It was Will's fault, she decided. Totally Will's fault.

Except that if I'm so angry with him it probably means he was right, and sleeping with him would have been a disaster. I'm too much of a mess to be dealing with this—with any sort of feeling for a man. I want it to *go away*!

CHAPTER SEVEN

'DID you manage to get through that paper?' Sarah
Jamieson asked Jennifer on Monday morning, drawing her
aside beyond one of the bulky monitors belonging to the
baby next to Teresa.

'Yes, I did,' Jennifer answered, adding with a generosity
that was a little hard to generate, 'And Dr Hartman was
right. It was excellent. Very clear and detailed.'

'He does seem to like my stuff.'

The resident gave a secretive, cat-like smile, which
brought Jennifer's goodwill to an abrupt end, and she
couldn't resist adding, and truthfully, too, 'If you're submit-
ting it to anyone important I did notice quite a few typos
and a couple of bits of dodgy grammar. I. . .er. . .marked
them in the copy you gave me in case they'd slipped by
your proof-reading.'

'I'm already aware of any errors,' Sarah said firmly.
'You needn't have bothered.'

'OK, then. No problem.'

'Look, while we have a minute—' Sarah was frowning
now '—there's something I've been wanting to say.'

'Yes?'

She gave a little laugh. 'Professional advice, I guess.'
She didn't wait for an acknowledgement from Jennifer but
went on quickly and decisively, 'You need to get your
feelings for Will Hartman under control. It's inappropriate
and it risks carrying you into some very dangerous waters.
It hasn't gone unnoticed—'

'*What* hasn't gone unnoticed?' Jennifer returned ominously.

'The way you look at him, respond to him, speak to him.' Sarah swept on. 'Do take my advice—it's well meant—and get your feelings under control. Realise that the sort of gratitude you feel towards him for what he's doing for Teresa is very natural and normal. . .'

'Well, yes, I'm grateful, of course.'

'But realise, too, that it's very transient. It's *not* reciprocated beyond the fact that he's flattered—which, again, is natural—but the danger of responding sexually to that form of hero-worship is something that a man like Will Hartman is very aware of. It's a commonly acknowledged professional risk, and you'll save yourself a lot of embarrassment and heartache if you don't force *him* to be the one to set limits.'

'Set limits?'

'I know he's looking after you somewhat more carefully than he'd look after most relatives of patients because of your unusual situation and your status as a fellow doctor. But don't read more into it than is meant, and don't attempt to take it any further. It's not a relationship between equals, as it might be if you were a colleague, and Will is absolutely not the sort of man to exploit an unequal power balance. I'm saying this because I do empathise with everything you're going through, and I understand how vulnerable it makes you.'

She finished at last.

Jennifer was left speechless. At first she had been furious. How dared this woman—who was her own age and would have been at the same professional level if Jennifer had been able to continue her own residency—presume to lecture to her in such a way? How dared she presume that her advice was wanted or *needed*? How dared she sound so confidently superior and so kindly patronising?

But as she really began to listen to the words they acquired a horrible ring of plausibility and good sense, and by the time Sarah finished Jennifer had started to see how well what she was saying fitted the facts.

Saturday night, too, she thought as she managed a faint nod and acknowledgement of Sarah's speech. It explains everything—explains exactly why he withdrew like that and wouldn't really explain. Will must have seen it too—my vulnerability, the danger of hero-worship, the impossibility of equality between us, the inappropriate acting out of transient desires—and that's why he withdrew.

'Thank you, Sarah,' she managed aloud at last. 'I'll—I'll think very carefully about what you've said.'

'Good!' The other woman's wide mouth spread in a satisfied smile. 'I'm glad you haven't taken offence. As I said, it's well meant and the sort of course correction I hope someone would help *me* with if I were ever in a similar situation. Now, if you'll excuse me. . .'

'Of course.'

Sarah bustled off to the opposite end of the unit, a heavy frown etched into her high forehead as she donned an aura of successfully doing six things at once. Jennifer couldn't help watching her curiously as she moved from baby to baby, and she began to realise that, actually, Sarah wasn't getting much done at all.

She was inefficient and didn't tackle her tasks in the right order. She wasted two pairs of gloves as she put them on only to compromise their sterility, by touching a soiled dressing or other item so that she had to pull them off and start again. She was clumsy, too, and messed up the insertion of an IV to the point where one of the nurses quietly took over. Then she almost created a wholesale panic by getting two babies' histories mixed up in her mind and announcing that Desean Johnson had lost 200 grams since Friday and should at once be put through a battery of tests.

'Dr Jamieson,' Jennifer heard Nurse Delia Washington say carefully, 'that's baby Johnson's chart you're looking at but this baby on the scales is Lequay Jackson and he's gaining well.'

There was a tiny silence, then Sarah said, 'Right. OK. Good. Then I'm supposed to be. . .'

'Assessing whether he can be weaned from the ventilator and go onto CPAP.'

'Sorry.' She laughed mechanically. 'Tired! The names are confusing, aren't they? Johnson and Jackson. And half these mothers just make up their babies' first names. Weird!'

'Some of the names are very nice,' Delia answered, rather frosty now.

Jennifer, as a result of several chats with this very experienced African-American nurse over the past few weeks, knew that her own sons were called Daquille and Tayrone so it wasn't very tactful of Sarah to criticise made-up names. The latter, however, tended to cocoon herself in that elaborate aura of busyness and never talked much with the nurses so she probably wasn't aware that Delia Washington even had any sons.

A moment later Jennifer had forgotten Sarah and her problems. There was a mild flurry at the entrance to the unit and there were Will Hartman and Keith Fitzgerald, which meant that Teresa was due for her eye exam.

Jennifer immediately lost all the strength in her legs. Will was looking at her, a searching, curious kind of look that she understood at once.

He's trying to work out if I'm OK, she thought. But is it the eye exam he thinks I'll be going to pieces over or *him*? After Saturday night. . .

He came up to her and said in a gravelly voice, 'Hi.' She felt the deliberate brush of his warm fingers against her hand, a gesture of support. 'How was Sunday?'

'Oh good,' she managed. 'I slept, ,swam. . .'

'I approve.'

'I spent about six hours in here between noon and six, and then came back again from eight till. . .I guess about eleven.'

'Did you give her her sponge-bath?' He smiled.

'Yep. Wouldn't miss that, would I? How about you? All those jars of pasta sauce and salsa safely sterilised and stored away?'

'Enough for a good six months, I think.'

'Makes me hungry.'

They smiled at each other again and she thought, This loss of strength. . .I hate it. It's him. What he does to me when he's this close and looking at me like that. I'm actually *not* nervous about the exam now.

Dr Fitzgerald wasn't wasting any time. He had stepped across to shake her hand and introduce himself. 'I understand you have a special interest in my area?'

She pulled herself together enough to say smoothly, so as not to tell an out and out lie, 'It's a fascinating field, and still advancing so fast. And, of course, I—I have a special interest in the baby,' she stressed. 'In Teresa, and what this exam means for her sight in the future.'

The appeal in her voice must have been very apparent as she forgot about Will and focused on the baby.

'I've done this innumerable times,' Dr Fitzgerald told her kindly.

'Oh, of course, and you must find it very rewarding to be able to implement new techniques and give sight to babies who a few years ago would have been bli—'

'Hush!' He cut her off quickly. 'We don't even say that word in my hearing.'

He was putting on his gloves, seeming eager to get to work with her as an audience. 'Now, the first thing I'm going to do. . .'

It was like a private lecture for her benefit and she was soon caught up in it, though it was hard not to react to Teresa's response. It wasn't painful for her but the lights were bright and that lid retractor, holding each eye open in turn, couldn't possibly feel good. Dr Fitzgerald used eye drops to dilate each pupil, then a special instrument to gently depress the white of the eye so that the entire retina could be seen through the pupil.

'What I need to see,' he explained now, in a rather droning tone that betrayed the degree of his concentration, 'is the orderly growth of blood vessels over the surface of the retina.' Then he was silent. The seconds ticked by, seeming to stretch endlessly. He spoke again, in that same focused murmur, 'And, unfortunately. . .' he was looking into the right eye '. . .I'm not seeing it.'

Jennifer gave a little cry. His tone was so calm and detached. She felt her strength ebbing again, and then there was a movement beside her and Will had come closer to take her elbow in a supportive grip. She was shaking now and he must be able to feel it.

'Steady,' he said very quietly. 'Let's hear the whole story.'

'There's definitely evidence of abnormal growth and scarring, to a degree which is producing retinal detachment.

That, as you know, is what we need to prevent or halt. I'll have her scheduled for tomorrow.'

'For. . .?' Jennifer asked Dr Fitzgerald on a croak.

'Cryosurgery,' he said briefly. 'I'll check the left eye now. Whichever is worst affected we'll tackle first, and the other eye a week later.'

He took the same careful look at Teresa's left eye. She was unhappy, crying her small cry, but not yet mature enough to know how to fight what was happening to her.

'That has to be hurting!' Jennifer exclaimed, then met an irritated stare from the ophthalmologist.

'It's not. Please let me complete the exam.'

'I'm sorry, I—'

Will's warm squeeze on her elbow told her not to distract the man further by overblown apologies.

'It's necessary, of course,' she said more firmly.

'The left eye is less affected,' Dr Fitzgerald announced after a few minutes, then rattled off a detailed technical description of the exact degree and type of damage which would scarcely have made sense to her, doctor though she was, if she hadn't read Sarah's paper over the weekend. 'So we'll do the right eye tomorrow,' he finished. 'Now, if you *do* want to be there. . .' His tone was slightly impatient.

She produced a brisk, controlled reply. 'Yes, I do. Now, she'll be paralysed for the procedure, won't she? As well as under general anaesthesia?'

'That's right.'

'It's incredible how non-invasive these new techniques are, of course. . .' It was very forced, but if Dr Fitzgerald was aware of this he didn't comment.

'Yes, although, of course, it does demand an enormous amount of control and concentration. It's not a procedure everyone can master.'

'I'll. . .look forward to seeing you at work, then.'

'Good!' He smiled and made a brisk movement away from Teresa's isolette, clearly already moving on to his next task—another eye exam on another preemie in the unit.

Half an hour later Jennifer was appalled at the stab of jealousy she felt when the mother of the second baby told her, 'We're to bring him for more check-ups over the next six months after he's discharged, but at this stage the reti—what's it. . .'

'Retinopathy,' Jennifer supplied.

'That's right. It's very mild.'

'Very mild, while Teresa might yet go blind. It was painfully, miserably unfair. She felt sick as she tried to keep this totally reprehensible envy from showing in her face and her voice and her body language, and congratulated the relieved, beaming parents.

The rest of the day dragged dreadfully. Teresa must have been stressed by the exam as she was looking paler than usual, with stiffened limbs and a decreased heart rate. Jennifer tried to soothe her with feather-light strokings and a light hand on her abdomen, but today this didn't seem to help. Finally Helen Bradwell said gently, 'Better stop. I know you want to tell her everything's OK now but I think she just needs to be left alone.'

So she just sat there for hours more. She forgot lunch and became stiff and headachy, wondering if the precious eyes shielded by their transparent reddish lids would ever see normally. The unit was its usual busy, noisy self, but she was oblivious to everything.

Oblivious, that was, until six o'clock when Will appeared and said with manufactured cheerfulness, only thinly overlaying his evident concern, 'Still here?'

She sat back and rubbed her neck. Teresa was due for

a feed. She could see Andrea Jones preparing a batch of them now for all the babies in the unit who were currently being fed by tube. Teresa's heart rate had gone up again and her colour had improved. With no memory or understanding of what had happened to her, it was as if Dr Fitzgerald's visit had never taken place.

'If only it was the same for me,' she thought, then realised that she'd actually mumbled the words aloud. As it didn't fit as an answer to what Will had just said he was looking more concerned still.

'Sorry,' she said. 'I've been in a daze.'

'I'm going to grab something to eat. Want to come?'

She made a face. 'Not sure if I could face the Monday cafeteria menu. For some reason, that's when they always seem to believe people crave pork. In large slabs.'

He laughed. 'Too true, which is why I'm heading down for Chinese at Campus Pizza. Please come!'

Surrendering control again, she went. She felt so wilted that she let him choose dishes for them both to share, top up her jasmine tea and even guide the conversation, which he soon brought round to what was on her mind.

'That was hard for you today.'

'I'd really been hoping she wouldn't need surgery. What's next, I wonder? She seems to be running the gamut.'

'She's doing very well, Jennifer.'

'To you it seems that way because she's one of dozens under your care. But to me, when I breathe every breath with her and when I'll be living with any long-term problems for years. . . You're just not tied to this like I am.'

'I might be more than you think,' he said, and laid a hand over hers on the table while they waited for the main course that followed their soup.

It was a close, comforting sort of gesture. Not threaten-

ing, just nice. And he must have seen in her face and in
the gradual drain of tension from her body that she liked it
and it was doing her good. Their silence now was intensely
nourishing, and she was achingly grateful to him for not
breaking it.

Of necessity, though, they couldn't linger over the meal.
He ate neatly but quickly, and she wanted to tell him,
Slow down! I've loved the times we've spent two hours
over dinner.

But she knew he couldn't tonight. He was on call. When
he polished off huge heaps of chicken fried rice and shrimp
with vegetables and Mongolian beef in record time she
could tell he was racing against the all-too-likely event of
his pager going off.

It didn't, though, and he finished his plateful, which
meant he at last seemed to feel he had the time to talk.
'Have you thought at all about your plans once Teresa is
discharged?'

'Discharged. . .' It seemed about as relevant as discussing
Teresa's choice of career. She blurted with painful humour,
'Well, I'd been thinking of steering her towards law.'

He caught her reference, and insisted, 'You know, it's
really not that far off. Six weeks. Less. With your medical
knowledge and your experience in caring for her, I'll be
looking at discharge when she reaches four pounds—
maybe even a little less. And I presume. . . Boston is your
intended home?'

'I did grow up there.'

'And Teresa will do the same.'

'I expect so.'

'You'll attempt to restart your residency year and put
her in a day care?'

'Unless she has special needs. In which case, I'd prob-

ably delay another year so that I can really focus on the
sort of therapy that will get her up to par developmentally.'

'She may not need it. She had none of the brain haemor-
rhaging that can cause neurological problems. And any
setbacks she has had, she's pulled through so well.'

'But this sight thing. . .'

'We keep coming back to it.'

'I'm sorry, I—'

'Don't be. It's what's on your mind.' His hand returned
to cover hers again. 'I just wish—'

He stopped, and she looked at him questioningly.
'Yes, Will?'

'Nothing. Finish because I need to get back.'

'I don't think I can. . .' She waved chopsticks at her
plate, daunted by what still remained.

He was holding something back. She was sure of it,
and this was robbing her of appetite. She couldn't help
remembering Sarah's speech today about power balance,
vulnerability, appropriate conduct and professional risk. It
seemed very likely that Will was thinking along the same
lines and she wanted to tell him, You don't have to worry.
I'm as aware as you are that our situation is too messy for
me to build anything real on this attraction. It's as substantial and trustworthy as a holiday romance. As long as you
don't kiss me. . .

But he *did* kiss her, outside the restaurant five minutes
later, his mouth hot and hungry and frustrated on hers and
his arms holding her so tightly that it was almost painful
because his pager had just gone off and there was no time
for this at all.

'Keep it,' he told her with rough, abstracted urgency.
'Keep that feeling of my mouth on yours. . .*please*!
Because *I'll* be keeping it, even if—Damn! There isn't

time to say this. They must have failed to stop labour on a woman they admitted this afternoon. If it *is* that she's only twenty-four weeks, unless her dates are wrong. . .'

He was already pulling her towards the car with rough speed.

It was a nightmare of a night, busy and understaffed. Nurse Louise Yoder was going through a divorce and had been less reliable lately. Tonight she turned up red-eyed and tight-mouthed, and then went off sick—and looking it—an hour into the shift. No replacement could be drummed up.

There were two very sick babies needing one-to-one care, and everyone knew that the twenty-four-weeker about to be delivered would soon be demanding their full attention—if the baby survived those first critical minutes in the delivery room with Will.

Teresa had recently made another of her many 'gradations', this time to being able to share a nurse with another baby. Tonight, because of the understaffing, this baby was Kenny Fugitt, a 'crack baby' whose condition was still touch-and-go. He needed a nurse to himself but it wasn't possible so he and Teresa shared. Inevitably, this brought Jennifer into a relationship with him that tore at her and turned her into a doctor again.

'Does Kenny's mum ever show up?' she asked young, efficient Cindy Lockyer when the latter had just shuttled across from the tiny boy to Teresa.

'Can't,' came the laconic and deliberately harsh response. 'She's dying of AIDS down at Novak House.' This was the AIDS hospice which was part of Riverbank, though situated a mile away.

Jennifer hissed a shocked response. Crack addiction,

AIDS. . . It happened, but it was always hard to confront it. 'And is the baby—?'

'HIV positive? too soon to say. He wasn't on his first test, but that's not conclusive yet, as you know. He may well be because the mother had no prenatal care, and they do believe now that some AIDS drugs given to the mother during pregnancy can drastically reduce the chance of transmitting the disease *in utero*. Well, you'd know that, too. . .'

'He's sweet. . .' Jennifer said.

'He's a problem, too. Lots of ups and downs. Gaining weight but. . .actually, look at his IV site. I think I'm going to have to change it yet again.'

Jennifer looked and nodded, seeing the problem at once. 'The infusion is leaking into the surrounding tissue.'

Cindy sighed. 'Well, I'll deal with it now. Things are quiet—for me, at least.' She looked across to where the team had just entered with the twenty-four-weeker—a girl—in her transport isolette. Her initial resuscitation had been successful, but everyone was aware that this was merely the first of an uncountable number of milestones.

Sarah Jamieson was there, stepping in now to start setting up IVs, monitors and plastic wrap to prevent fluid loss through the skin.

Cindy whistled, looking at the new arrival. 'Man, she is *small*!'

Jennifer caught sight of Will's bleak expression as he stood back and left these next steps to his residents, and thought, He doesn't think she's going to make it. He's *hoping* she won't because the likelihood of long-term problems is so great. If Teresa had been born ten days earlier, or even seven, she would have been the same. I shouldn't panic about tomorrow. Teresa is lucky. . .

Meanwhile, Kenny Fugitt wasn't.

'This vein does *not* look great,' Cindy was saying. 'I don't think. . . Dr Hartman?' she called tentatively, but he had joined in the fray again. He was almost shouting at Kyle Reeve, another of the residents, 'No, you can't turn the setting up that high! You'll blow a hole in her lung. She has to make it on the setting you've got now.'

Cindy turned to Jennifer. 'Look, what do you think? Is this vein going to take multiple fluids? It's so fragile but there just aren't any more veins.'

Jennifer came over. 'You're right, I think. It's going to be too much. Can you alternate the infusions?'

'I'll need a doctor to write up new orders.' She glanced down the unit again, and they both heard Will say, 'No, I'm not prepared to tie up our one oscillator on this baby when we're about to have a twenty-five-weeker with a better prognosis to whom it might be more real use.'

'We're about to have a twenty-five-weeker?' Cindy muttered. 'Who's "we"?'

'I'm calling again for emergency nursing cover,' said Faith McConnell, who was running the staffing of the unit on this shift. 'We *really* need someone now!'

'Dr Jamieson. . .?' Cindy steered her way through the machines to where Sarah had now detached herself from the group of staff around the new baby.

She looked shaken and strained, and said rather blankly, 'Yes, what is it?'

'I need you to write new orders for Baby Fugitt's infusion.'

'God, not *now*! Why?'

Cindy explained about the dearth of suitable veins, and about Jennifer's suggestion that the two types of nutritional fluids little Kenny was receiving intravenously be alternated.

'Do you really think that's necessary? *I* don't!'

She glanced irritatedly at Jennifer, then studied the chart and the baby. 'Look, I'll do it later if I have to. For now, carry on mixing them, OK?'

'No, it's *not* OK,' Cindy muttered mutinously when Sarah had gone back to the new admission. 'She'll realise it when she has a minute. I'm going to do it, anyway, and get her to write up the order later.'

'That's. . .' Jennifer began.

'I know. Not protocol. But we're short-staffed and over-booked. If another baby's on its way. . .'

She deftly manipulated IV tubing and syringes to start infusing the first of the nutritional supplements that Baby Fugitt received. He was also on two-hour stomach feeds by nasogastric tube, and the next of those was due at ten.

Faith McConnell came by again and suggested to Cindy, 'If you've got a minute make up the ten o'clock feeds for all the babies. Gina's rattling around with four to deal with and no one else is any better off. Can you manage it?'

'Sure. . .'

The efficient young nurse found an odd corner and started preparing feed syringes, muttering under her breath and ticking off names on a list. Then she went round the unit like a beneficent fairy, dispensing her goodies to the eight babies on tube feeds. She'd done it so promptly that the feeds were not yet quite due so each syringe with its white fluid sat ready beside each isolette, including Teresa's.

'She's starting to wake. Is she getting on a schedule, I wonder?' Jennifer murmured, focusing on her own particular baby and forgetting about the drama of the other babies for now. 'Do you know it's coming soon, love?'

There were distinct snufflings going on, and grimaces

and stirrings. She'd start to cry fairly soon—the little mewling sound that was getting stronger every day.

In the background of her awareness she heard Faith McConnell say to Cindy Lockyer, 'There isn't anyone. Some bug is going round and everyone's sick, it seems. Can I give you Baby Mann as well because Jennifer's with Teresa, which frees you up a little?'

'Sure.' Cindy nodded. 'Jennifer won't let anything happen.'

In hindsight, the words seemed painfully, ironically wrong.

Things had quietened a little now. It was still twenty minutes until the ten o'clock feed, the twenty-five-weeker that people were talking about was holding off being born for a little longer and Will had actually deemed it possible to retire to an on-call room. Sarah came over, but Jennifer didn't really notice her until she heard her angry voice from beside Kenny Fugitt's isolette.

'You had something to do with this, didn't you, Jennifer?'

'What?' She was too dazed to phrase it more elegantly. She'd been absorbed in Teresa.

'You got Cindy to alternate this baby's infusions when I'd written no such orders. Didn't you?'

'Look, I supported her opinion that that's what should be done, but I—'

A bell rang, summoning the triage team urgently to Labour and Delivery. It must be the twenty-five-weeker at last.

Sarah said impatiently, 'I'm on the team for the delivery room this time. I can't stay.' She thrust a syringe of white fluid into Jennifer's hand. 'Here. Add this to the infusion or I really will have you thrown off the unit. You had no business to give any sort of opinion to Cindy, especially not one that directly contradicted my own orders. The infusion rate can be slowed if necessary, but I don't think we need to muck around alternating the fluids. Now, put it in! You've *got* to, because I have *no* time!'

Shakily, Jennifer did so, wondering if she should take the initiative to slow the rate herself but deciding against it. She didn't agree with what Sarah was doing, but with no official role here she felt her hands were tied. Even this simple task of attaching the syringe to the IV line was not something she was authorised to do.

And at ten o'clock she discovered that she'd done something far worse than merely flouting protocol.

'Where's his NG feed?' Cindy said, returning to Kenny's isolette. 'It was right here by the—' she broke off. '*And what's this second syringe being infused*?'

She met Jennifer's gaze and there was dawning horror in both of them.

'Sarah grabbed the feed syringe,' Jennifer whispered. 'She...she pushed it into my hand and told me to attach it. I didn't check, and neither did she. Oh, my God, we're infusing a stomach feed straight into his veins!'

'Not all that much has gone in,' Cindy said. Cutting across her words came the electronic keening of the apnoea alarm. She flicked the baby's heel to prompt him to breathe again, then pulled the syringe from the IV line and closed the tap. 'Maybe...maybe it won't be a problem,' she whispered, but it was obvious that she didn't believe it even as she said it. Neither did Jennifer. 'Let's ask Dr Jamieson if—'

'No! Page Dr Hartman,' Jennifer returned. 'Sarah's in a delivery and, anyway—'

'It's her fault!'

'No, it's mine. I should have—'

'Don't argue. There isn't time. *I* don't know what to do.'

'N-neither do I.'

Will did, though. He arrived within a minute of being paged.

'We'll aspire it back into the tube as much as we can first,' he said, 'then we'll flush him with fluids, try and dilute it out.'

'And if. . .if it doesn't work?' Jennifer managed.

'Then there's a serious risk of fat embolism.'

'Because we've actually infused globs of fat straight into his veins, and if they get stuck further along. . .' Cindy outlined graphically.

Nobody needed to hear it put quite like that. Jennifer shuddered and felt sick. She had done this with her own hands!

'We'll also stand by to put him on bypass, if necessary,' Will was saying now.

'You mean we'll do a complete exchange of blood?' Again it was Cindy, zeroing in on the most graphic way of putting it.

Will nodded. 'As a last resort. If we get to that point. . .' He didn't finish. Clearly, he thought that if Baby Fugitt needed this treatment he might be beyond the point where it would do him any good, and to have it almost voiced like this—that he could die. . .

And there's nothing I can do, Jennifer realised as she shrank back out of the way while Cindy, Will, Sarah and a second nurse, Judy Lawrence, worked over the baby. The aspiration of the vein produced a small amount of white fluid but there had to be more still in there and Will wasted no time before ordering the baby's IV bag filled and set to flow at the fastest rate the tiny system could stand.

Sarah was in charge of setting up the equipment for bypass which she did in an angry, ostentatious way, as if to make it quite clear that she would solve this crisis even though she didn't feel she had caused it.

Meanwhile, Judy kept a running commentary on Kenny's vital signs, which grated on Jennifer like chalk on a blackboard although she knew it was necessary. Miraculously, as time passed, she realised that those vital signs were remaining stable.

'I don't think we'll need the bypass now,' Will said in the early hours of the morning, returning to the baby after an hour's absence dealing with other patients.

'Is. . .is he out of danger yet?' Cindy ventured.

'It's starting to look that way.'

'That's—that's so good!' Jennifer breathed.

'How did it happen?' The mild query dropped into the weary quiet like a stone dropping into a still, deep pond. . . and created as many ripples. Jennifer looked at Cindy, and Cindy looked at Sarah. Sarah was currently very occupied, briskly writing in Baby Fugitt's chart, and she didn't look up as she said coolly, 'Perhaps you'd like to explain, Jennifer?'

'I—'

'It wasn't really Jennifer's fault,' Cindy supplied at once. This didn't help.

'How could it be Jennifer's fault?' Will asked ominously. 'She has no role here, other than as Teresa's guardian. Just what exactly is being suggested?'

He was looking at her now, his dark eyes complex and unreadable in what they expressed. Clearly, he wanted an explanation that would let her off the hook. Unfortunately, there wasn't one.

'I was the one who. . .actually attached the wrong syringe,' she began.

It was a fault, clearly, but Sarah was surely more to blame! Jennifer hated being the one to have to introduce the story and understood how hard it would be for a woman like Sarah to have to confess to such a series of mistakes— ignoring the tissuing of fluid around the IV site, downplaying the unsuitability of the new vein, refusing to take action to deal with the problem. . .

Except that Sarah's resolute silence soon betrayed that she wasn't planning to confess to anything at all. Jennifer looked at her—glared, in fact, to prompt her—but nothing came, and Will was echoing, horrified and angry. '*You* attached the syringe?'

'Yes.'

'Why?'

'Because. . .' Sarah, you *have* to say something at this point.

Silence.

'Because I didn't check,' Jennifer continued doggedly, 'that it was the right one.'

'You had no authority to be touching any such syringe in the first place.'

'I know.' Her teeth clenched. Should she involve Sarah?

The other woman was staring at her, her golden-brown eyes rounded and beseeching. 'This is *my career*,' she mouthed.

Cindy came in urgently, 'Dr Hartman, you must hear the full story. It began with Kenny's IV leaking fluid into the surrounding tissue, and when I asked Dr—'

'I'm not sure I need to hear it tonight, do I?' he interrupted. 'We're all beat and we still have a crowded unit and dangerously thin staffing for the rest of the night. If there's more to the story than I've heard I'll hear it—coherently, please—in the morning. He's going to live and, Jennifer. . .?'

'Yes?'

'No matter what urgent problem you thought you were dealing with you shouldn't have been. You should have called someone. OK?'

'I—Yes.' She nodded firmly. 'OK.'

He was right about one thing. They didn't have time for this now. Baby Mann's monitor was going off and Nurse Leah Cohen from the 'growers and feeders' section of the unit was yelling for a doctor.

'Go home, Jennifer,' Will said. *Ordered*, in fact, in a tired, reproachful voice.

'I—I am.' And I'll deal with this tomorrow, after Teresa's eye surgery, because it can't end like this.

CHAPTER EIGHT

MY BABY is paralysed.

In the operating room, throughout the two-hour cryosurgery procedure, this was all Jennifer could think of. She knew it was a deliberately induced, completely controlled and temporary thing, brought about by medication, but to see Teresa so totally immobile and herself become paralysingly haunted by the irrational fear that somehow the tiny baby's ability to move would not return. . .

'I'm now going to begin touching the probe to each blood vessel in order to freeze it, passing directly through the outer surface of the eye,' Keith Fitzgerald droned, and she knew it was for her benefit as he continued with a more technical description of what he was doing.

But she couldn't focus.

Teresa is paralysed.

'It's. . .it's amazing that surgery can be done like this,' she managed. 'So completely detailed and precise.'

And taking so long! It feels like for ever! What if I faint? I had so little sleep. . . Dr Fitzgerald would be furious, and I don't want him furious because how can he concentrate properly if he's furious? I mustn't faint! I won't! She bit the inside of her cheeks to keep herself alert and awake.

The minutes ticked by. 'If you did both eyes at once. . .' she murmured.

Dr Fitzgerald frowned. 'A three-hour procedure? Perhaps more?' he said. 'Far too much for a baby this size!'

'Of course.' It was reasonable and medically sound, but

it meant that she and Teresa had to go through this again a week from now.

At least next week she wouldn't be so tired and raw after the horror of last night. Kenny Fugitt's condition was continuing to improve after his close brush with death but that didn't undo what had so nearly been a fatally disastrous mistake, and she knew Will would need to hear the full story.

He wasn't present at the surgery this morning, and she hadn't seen Sarah since last night either.

After Dr Fitzgerald had completed his delicate work she stayed with Teresa through her time in Recovery and then came with her back up to the NICU, entering the unit with the orderly, Nurse Helen Bradwell and the transport isolette just as Will and Sarah arrived there together. Will's face was closed and brooding but Sarah looked radiant, her severe, Amazonian beauty more apparent today despite the fatigue around her eyes.

'Everything all right?' Will murmured to Jennifer as their paths crossed, but his tone was totally professional and he immediately passed on to look at all the other babies who warranted his special concern.

It wasn't until an hour later that he asked to speak to her privately. She was still hovering over Teresa's isolette when he came over. The baby was safely over the worst effects of the general anaesthesia, but the induced paralysis would take twenty-four hours to wear off completely and there was no sign of it doing so yet.

'She's doing fine,' were his first words, but they were mechanical, the sort of perfunctory reassurance that he generally managed to avoid.

'Dr Fitzgerald seemed pleased with how the surgery went. It's too soon to tell, of course.' She was only parroting

the paediatric ophthalmologist. 'She may need more surgery when she's older, and various forms of treatment—
exercises, glasses—to strengthen her vision.'

'We need to talk,' he said abruptly as soon as she had
finished. Today he wasn't standing close enough for her
to feel his warmth, and yet she was still aware of him.

'I know,' she answered. 'Conference room?'

'How about my office? I'd like to get right away from
the unit.'

She had never seen it. Neither, she suspected, had many
of the staff. It was only a cubby-hole, and clearly not a
place he liked to be very much, lacking the special touch
of peace and comfort that he'd worked so hard to give his
home. He even had to take a heap of file folders off the
second chair for her to sit down.

'I expect you want to hear—' she began, but he cut
her off.

'No, not a blow-by-blow account. Sarah's told me. She's
taken some of the blame, of course, as she was overseeing
Kenny's care. Cindy, too, although, like all of us last night,
she was grossly overloaded. But at bottom it was your
mistake, and that's particularly bad since it wasn't even a
job you should have been doing.'

'I know that, but—'

'Jennifer. . .' It was a plea, made in mixed tones of anger
and disappointment. 'You're not going to try and excuse
it, are you?'

'No, I'm not, but—'

'Look, in view of the complexity of the situation and
the fortunate outcome, in that Kenny's still with us, I'm
not going to take any action on this, but I must absolutely
tell you that you are not, under any circumstances, ever to
perform any sort of treatment or procedure on any patient

in this unit again. Looking through Teresa's chart and giving her her sponge-baths is one thing, but a patient with whom you have no connection—'

'I know that, Will,' she told him tightly. 'I know it, OK? And. . .thanks for letting it go at that.' It was cold comfort, actually, that he wasn't taking any official action.

She wondered what he'd said to Sarah, and would have liked to have known if there was any more official reprimand in her case—if it would go into her file somewhere. But she couldn't ask, of course, nor could she expect him to further muddy the waters of her own difficult position in the unit by telling her the substance of what he'd said to the other woman.

A moment later he echoed the conclusion she was just beginning to reach on her own. 'Look, perhaps ultimately it's for the best that something like this has happened. It will serve as a reminder to both of us. . .' he hesitated '. . .that we have to keep within certain boundaries. My role here is professional—yours isn't. That's not an insignificant difference in status.'

'Yes,' she answered, finding her voice with difficulty. 'We've known it all along, I think, but sometimes emotions can be deceptive and can get out of control.'

'They can,' he agreed crisply.

They were both thinking of it—vulnerability, heightened feeling, the shared experience of similar tragedies, transient but powerful awareness. It was there in the air between them even now. Right now, she could stand up and go to him, put her arms around his neck and turn her face up for his kiss, murmur the pleading truth that she needed him—needed his touch and support and sensuality—and she knew he'd given it to her.

But it was time to be stronger than that.

She *did* stand but didn't go to him, just said, firm and pleasant in her tone, 'Thanks, Will. I—I have a sense now that the worst of all this is over. It should be easier in future.'

'Yes,' he agreed. 'Let's hope so.'

She left quickly, preferring to assume that he didn't want to accompany her back to the unit. She deliberately stayed away from the hospital altogether after lunch and went to a movie, swam in the motel pool, then did some reading for a couple of hours in her room from a book on paediatrics that didn't even cover the subject of prematurity.

Before dinner, though, she dropped in to be with Teresa for a while and check that the paralysis was wearing off exactly as it should, and there were Will and Sarah, just leaving the unit together.

The latter still had that gorgeous, happy look on her face. She was wearing make-up, too, which she didn't always, and it brought out the boldly defined beauty of her features—the wide mouth, the high forehead, the large tawny brown eyes and thick lashes.

'Oh, but I *love* that restaurant, Will,' Jennifer heard. 'It wouldn't be a hardship to eat there again at all!'

Seeing her, they both smiled and said hello. Then they moved on towards the elevator, still talking. It was very clear that they were two trained professionals, sensibly and easily shrugging off the demands of their working day in order to enjoy their private lives—together for this evening, by the sound of it. And why shouldn't they? Sure, every baby in the unit was important to them, but none was a cause for agonised crying, wild moments of optimism and happiness or desperate prayers.

For the first time since coming to this hospital over six weeks ago Jennifer felt loneliness and a deep sense of isolation. She had had the illusion that Will was going through this with her, sharing what she felt, but he wasn't, of course. How could he?

Suddenly, it was an unbridgeable gap between them.

'She is my little Miss Incredible at the moment, aren't you, love?' crooned Helen Bradwell as she detached Teresa's feed syringe. 'Did you see what she weighed this morning, Jennifer?'

'No, I haven't checked her chart today.'

She was making a conscious effort to stay away a little more these days—do a little more for herself, including medical reading and exercising for a good hour each day. Not that this meant she was neglecting Teresa but rather that she was spending eight to ten hours here each day instead of sixteen or more.

It was a week now since Teresa's second eye surgery and Dr Fitzgerald was pleased, as was Will. In many ways, though, it was the opinion of the nurses that counted most, Jennifer had come to realise. Nurses such as Helen, who had been assigned to Teresa on every shift she had worked for the past eight weeks—since Teresa's birth. It wasn't surprising that many of the nurses cried when special babies that they might have spent months caring for were finally discharged.

Not that discharge was in close view yet for Teresa, but another milestone *would* take place today.

'Dr Hartman said you could hold her properly when she reached 1500 grams,' Helen was saying. 'And guess what?

'She did? She is?'

'She *just* tipped it this morning. . . Well, 1490, actually, but I'm going to cheat a bit. Would you like to?'

'*Like* to?' Jennifer retorted, her throat already tight. 'I'd. . . I'd. . .' She couldn't finish.

She had held Teresa before, in a fashion—giving her her sponge-bath inside the isolette or helping her on and off the scales when she was weighed. She'd touched her daily, too, those feather-light massages with her fingers. But that wasn't what Helen Bradwell meant. This time she meant *really* holding her, swaddled in a soft blanket and snuggled right up against her chest.

It was a painfully wonderful time. Teresa was so tiny that the blanket still felt almost empty, but she was warm and she moved, and when that tiny black head came to fit so snugly between Jennifer's breasts she was laughing and crying at the same time and had to struggle to keep calm enough to take the proper care.

She held Teresa for ten minutes, bending her head to listen to the rapid fragile puff of her breathing. She kissed her hands and her forehead and her cheeks, and sang to her softly. When she finished the second of the three lullabies she could call to mind at that moment she heard a soft masculine voice just behind her left shoulder.

'Does it feel good?'

It was Will, coming round so he could see properly and smiling at her.

She nodded, and felt heat rise through her. They hadn't seen much of each other over the past two weeks, and she knew that this avoidance was as deliberate on his part as it was on hers. They both recognised the necessity for it, but she suspected that she was the only one to recognise how lonely she felt now. *He* couldn't be lonely. He had his profession, the friends with whom he played his music and—increasingly, it seemed—he had Sarah Jamieson.

This provided him with a far more 'appropriate'—to

quote Sarah herself—relationship than anything he could have had with the guardian and adoptive parent of one of his patients. Sarah seemed determined that the new state of things should be openly known in the unit, too. She made a point of mentioning their dinners and outings together, praising a restaurant or a concert and reminiscing aloud with him over a delectable dish or a brilliant performance.

Will didn't altogether seem to share this need to discuss their affair, but neither did he deny that they were spending time together. He was a healthy, normal man, after all. He must have had relationships since Amy's death ten years ago, and it seemed that this was going to be one of them.

Jennifer couldn't help feeling that Sarah must be burning the candle at both ends, though. She was, after all, in the middle of demanding residency, and she always seemed so harassed and frazzled as she strode around the unit—less so, perhaps, when Will himself was in evidence, as if she was determined not to let him see that she wasn't coping.

Hang on. . . Not coping? Was that too strong? Perhaps, although twice Jennifer had overheard Sarah beseeching one of the other residents, Kyle Reeve, to cover for her the following night, and she'd do it for him next month when she was on top of things again.

Both times the other resident had agreed but with an uneasy intonation, as if not quite convinced that the favour would ever be returned. Jennifer wondered if Will kept a close enough track of the on-call schedule to realise that this was what Sarah was doing. Then it occurred to her that perhaps he had suggested the idea in the first place in order to have her company for an evening.

But surely that wasn't his style. . .

He was still watching her with Teresa, a warm, intent look on his face and a crooked smile—as if it really did give him pleasure to see this Madonna-and-child moment. And she couldn't help wanting him to know just how right this felt.

'I—I've been worried, in my darker moments, Will,' she told him softly, the words tumbling out. 'Worried that this wouldn't feel right, that I wouldn't feel like her mother and wouldn't know what to do. But I *do* know, and it's so wonderful. Look at how contented she is! As if she knows, despite spending so much time with Helen and Andrea and Allie and Sharon, that *I'm* the one who's going to be around for ever.'

'Of course she knows,' he answered. 'How could she not know? It's been there from the beginning in every moment you've spent with her, every stroking touch you've given her through the ports of the isolette and every word you've spoken or note you've sung. Of course she knows! And she knows how lucky she is, too. That's why she's growing so fast now.'

'You really believe that?'

'Well, I could produce studies and statistics and replace all the short, common-sense words for it with long, incomprehensible ones but, yes, you know it's generally acknowledged now that there's a positive physiological response to the sensation of being touched and loved.'

'She's so beautiful!'

She wasn't. Not really. Not yet.

Teresa was still far too small and thin and red and frog-like, with that indefinable aura of great age and weariness that tiny babies have, even full-term ones, and Jennifer could see all this herself when she looked at Teresa with the determinedly objective eyes of a doctor. But at the moment she wasn't thinking that way at all, and because Teresa was so very strongly loved there was a deeper truth to the words and she *was* beautiful.

Will pressed his lips together tightly, then suddenly turned away to clear his throat. 'Well, I have a group of students. . .'

'OK, well, I guess—' She was about to say something casual about seeing him later but he had already gone, his back rather tight and stiff somehow.

'We'd better put her back now and set up her feed,' Helen said.

'Will I get longer tomorrow?' Jennifer asked wistfully.

'Hope so. Let's see if this seems to have tired her.'

'I think she loved it.'

'I think so, too.'

All the indications were that Teresa *had* loved it, and within a week Jennifer was holding her for an hour at a time as her weight steadily climbed and she made more of those vital preemie 'gradations'. She was one of the 'feeders and growers' now, and she was ready to learn to drink from a bottle.

Kathy Solway was still faithfully and generously donating her breast-milk. It had matured and changed in composition but Will agreed with Jennifer that it would still be the best form of nourishment for Teresa. With more ability now to think beyond the world of the NICU, Jennifer was finding ways to thank Kathy for her generosity in providing this service.

She babysat twice so that the Solways could go out to dinner together, although Kathy was too nervous to leave Andrew for more than an hour and a half so both times it was a quick meal. She bought several outfits for the baby— outfits which seemed huge to her, although they were the smallest newborn size. And she dropped off baskets of gourmet foods, for which Kathy was particularly grateful.

'Because the day just *goes*, and I don't get a thing done. Shopping or cooking. . . How on earth do people manage with two? Or *three*?'

'Or nine!' Jennifer agreed.

There had been a ninth child in the unit for a couple of days but his problems had been minor and he'd gone home, to leave Jennifer thinking the same as Kathy and wondering how on earth people did manage.

She wondered this again on the first auspicious day when Helen Bradwell told her that it was time to try bottle-feeding because something that sounded so straightforward and not particularly time-consuming—sitting with Teresa in her arms and holding a special preemie nipple to her mouth—turned out to be not straightforward at all and took an hour and a half.

'Is it me?' she asked Helen miserably after the first ten minutes.

'No, honey, not really. It's her. This is tiring for her and she doesn't know what she's supposed to be doing so she shirks her job by going off to sleep, naughty thing.'

'I'm tempted to say, "Here, *you* do it." '

'Well, you can if you like.'

'No, because, really, after all this time to be actually caring for her myself. . .it's so good!' She whisked away a tear or two.

'OK, well, she's opened her eyes again now. Try just brushing the tip of the nipple across her lips. . .there!'

'She sucking. . . Now she's gagging.'

'It's coming too fast. The hole must be too big. Try tilting her up a little—No? Not working, is it?' Helen made a face. Milk was running from the corner of Teresa's mouth. 'That's a nuisance after she's got such a nice grip on the nipple. We'll have to pull it out and fit a new one to the bottle. Now, to break the suction just gently put the tip of your finger into the corner of her mouth. At this stage you could hurt her just by pulling and breaking the suction too roughly.'

And so it went on. Teresa sucked for a few minutes on a nipple that had the right rate of flow, then got tired and went to sleep again. Jennifer tried to prod her awake by jiggling the bottle a little, and she gave one more sleepy suck then drifted off again.

'Let's wait a bit,' Helen suggested.

'Can I keep holding her?'

'She looks good so I don't see why not.'

After nearly an hour Teresa had woken and this time managed to finish the feed, which then heralded the next impossible task—burping her. The air bubble did eventually come up, along with what looked to Jennifer like most of the feed.

Helen promised her it wasn't. 'It's like when my kids spill orange juice,' she said. 'There's always ten times more on the floor than there could possibly have been in the cup in the first place.'

Slowly it got easier. Jennifer wasn't always there to give a feed and Teresa's nurses, who were so experienced at this, soon came up with various positions and tricks that worked best, which they then helped Jennifer herself to master. Teresa's weight gain slowed and almost stopped for her first week on bottle-feeding, but then it slowly began to pick up again.

The hot summer weather came to an end, and quite suddenly, too. One day it was a dirty, steamy ninety-two degrees, and then overnight a cool, fresh stream of air blew in from Canada, the muggy white sky became a brilliant blue and autumn had arrived.

'She'll be going home by the end of the month,' the nurses began to promise.

It was frightening, wonderful thought, and it brought with it a realisation that Jennifer would have to plan her own future. Would she go back to medicine? How had this experience shaped her?

They weren't questions that she hurried to answer, recognising that she still needed time to test any feelings that seemed so strong at the moment. But she started to observe more, and to be curious about just what it was that made a good doctor.

Jerry Gaines, for example. Was he good? He was difficult to work with. The nurses didn't like him much, but the parents were generally pleased because he acted like a cross between a super-hero and a movie star, dazzling them with a wide smile and performing with a flourish so that they noticed the heroism of his procedures.

It could have backfired disastrously if he hadn't truly known what he was doing but he did so Jennifer conceded that he *was* a good doctor even though she shared the nurses' opinion of his personality. Far too brash for her taste.

And how about Kyle Reeve? Like Sarah Jamieson he was a resident and was the one whom Sarah had prevailed upon to take her on-call two or three times, perhaps because he looked as if he *could* be prevailed upon in such a way. He had a boyish, rather shy-looking face and always thought so carefully about what he did that it sometimes came across as uncertainty.

Again, though, Jennifer considered him a good doctor. He cared, he was thorough, he had a wonderful knack for explaining things to some of the parents who seemed particularly at sea and if he really decided he didn't know then he always brought in someone who *did* know before it was too late.

Someone like Will, who would say, 'Good, Kyle.' He would then take over the problem, explaining what he was doing as he did it so that the next time it happened Kyle got it right.

And Will himself? Was he good?

That went without saying. His only blind spot seemed to be Sarah because, as far as Jennifer was concerned, she *wasn't* good. She had had her paper published, though, and was at work on another one, which somehow necessitated a lot of talk on the subject with Will—usually just before lunch so that they ended up heading off for the cafeteria together.

Why couldn't Will see, though, that all her talent and skill were on paper?

Even Kyle Reeve could see it. Jennifer was sitting quietly in the 'growers and feeders' section of the unit one night, giving Teresa her ten o'clock feed—still a rather tricky and time-consuming task—when she heard the two residents whispering over a moderately ill preemie's isolette nearby.

'That's *not* right, Sarah,' Kyle said insistently.

His voice rose a little, and when Jennifer glanced across at him she could see that his face wore a frustrated, anxious and unhappy look, as if he simply wished that this whole thing was happening to someone else.

'It *is* right! What's wrong with it?' Sarah was saying.

'You haven't worked out the dose right for her weight. You haven't allowed for the fact that she's on—' His voice dropped so that Jennifer couldn't hear any more but she saw Sarah nod after a few moments, as if finally conceding that Kyle was right.

This seemed to give him added confidence because now

his voice rose again and Jennifer heard, 'And it's not the first time it's happened so check your stuff and get it right the next time, *please*, because I shouldn't have to cover for you like this!'

It was pleading and angry at the same time, like a younger brother who has been asked to lie about his sister's where-abouts after school once too often and is on the point of rebelling and telling tales.

After she had finished Teresa's feed and was about to go back to her motel for the night Jennifer saw Kyle again working over the moderately ill Baby Slaley and couldn't help going up to him.

'Sarah didn't stuff up, did she?'

Kyle made a face. 'Almost. In theory, she knows a lot. We've crammed together for exams and, *boy*, does she know a lot! But when it comes to actual practice and actual patients. . .' He whistled and did a flapping motion with his hands. 'Out the window! She was about to give this kid totally the wrong dose of—'

He stopped suddenly, as if remembering that Jennifer wasn't a fellow resident here. His tone changed. 'Anyway, it wasn't a problem. Don't worry about it, uh, Jennifer.'

'OK,' she answered, not wanting to push. He wouldn't say any more now.

The incident frightened her, though. Teresa was doing so well. If Sarah. . .or anyone, of course. . .made a mistake and something went wrong. . .

Unofficially the nurses had talked about discharge but now even Will was using the word, albeit in a reserved kind of way as if he didn't quite want to commit himself.

'I'm going on vacation in a week, Jennifer,' he said, on the morning after the incident between Kyle and Sarah.

'We may even look at discharge before I go.'

'That's . . .That's. . .' She tried to feel pleased. Surely she *should* be ecstatic, despite some natural nervousness about being in sole charge of such a tiny baby. But she couldn't. For some reason, his words opened a frightening picture of emptiness very soon in the future.

It's him, she realised miserably. I won't see *him* any more, and that's horrible. I can't be in love with him. . .I don't trust anything I feel these days. . . But he's been so important to Teresa. . .and to me. . .and now it's just going to *end*!

She almost wished—*almost*—that he'd said Teresa should stay a little longer. She even said to him, 'But with the fact that I'll be travelling to Boston doesn't that mean she should stay here until she's just a bit stronger?'

'Travelling to Boston.' He frowned. 'Straight away?'

'Well, I guess I could—and perhaps I *should*—stay on in the motel for a couple of days, just to make sure I really know what I'm doing with her.'

His brow cleared. 'Yes. Yes, do. For a couple of weeks, even.'

That sounded lonely and difficult, too, though. I wish he'd keep her in until he gets home from vacation, came the fleeting, guilty wish, and she felt badly punished for it two days later.

Teresa developed a fever.

Probably nothing, everyone said. Babies this small just get fevers and sometimes we never even work out why. Don't worry, they all told us. But of course Jennifer *did* worry. Cultures were taken—blood, sputum and urine. Teresa's ears were checked and her throat was looked at. Her vitals were monitored more frequently. She was given the minute dose of medication that befitted her body weight to bring her fever down.

And in the end, after three days—as everyone had said— all her cultures came back negative and the fever left her.

All the same, Will pronounced, 'We'll put back her discharge by a couple of weeks. She's lost ground a little and she won't have reached a safe weight by the original date we discussed. I'm. . .sorry, Jennifer.'

'It's all right,' she told him. 'It. . .uh. . .gives me a little more time to prepare.' And a little more time with you.

But, of course, he was going away in just two days. No one knew where. He wasn't saying.

'Personal policy. He never does,' Helen Bradwell told Jennifer. 'There are rumours, of course.'

'Like the ones about him living in his car?'

'Yes.' Helen laughed. 'Although I don't think anyone actually believes those. Particularly over the past couple of months. He's loosened up somehow. There's a softer, less driven look to him. The vacation rumours, though. . .'

'What, he folds himself into a coffin like Count Dracula?' Jennifer suggested facetiously.

'No, but the idea that he's secretly married to some high flyer with a career in Chicago or New York has a strong following,' Helen answered. 'Personally, I think he goes to the Caribbean, picks a beach and lies on it for eighteen hours a day, fourteen days in a row. Its what *I'd* do in his position.'

'Have you decided yet on what you're going to do when you leave here?'

Jennifer knew that Helen had given in her notice to take effect a couple of weeks from now.

'Yes, I have, actually,' Helen answered briskly. 'I'm going to do home day care for a while, taking just two or three babies or toddlers with special needs. I'm so dread-fully attached to these babies, which is a *problem* here since they all eventually leave to go home—or if they don't that's even worse. But if I looked after a couple at home I'd get to actually play with them and see them starting to thrive and smile and develop. It'll take me a few more weeks to get it organised.

'Our house has to pass inspection and I have to get a home day care licence. But I think it'll nourish me for a few years until I feel ready—because I do *want* to feel ready—to come back to this again.'

There were other changes in the wind, too. Both Sarah and Kyle were due to move to a new rotation, Kyle to the children's ICU and Sarah to paediatric oncology. It wasn't hard to tell that she dreaded it, although she didn't actually say so. Her woeful insensitivity to parents in crisis seemed to be getting worse, and if she was tired she was really unbearable. . .except when Will was around.

He was on call tonight but wasn't in the unit for the moment. It was nine o'clock on the Thursday night two days before he was due to take off—either to his vampire coffin, his secret wife or his Caribbean island. Still no one knew which. Sarah *was* in the unit, though, for her last on-call before her new rotation.

It was unusually quiet. There had been several discharges over the past week and only one new admission so staff ranks were thinned by people, taking time off that they'd been owed for a while. There were groups of isolettes and warming tables corralled in corners that had been in use a week or two ago.

Even though it was unusually quiet, as this was a big unit that still meant lots of babies and lots of focused care. Baby Wright, born a week ago, was giving trouble tonight.

He was down the other end, where the smallest and sickest babies were kept, but Jennifer could still hear his apnoea alarm going off at intervals. He'd been weaned from the ventilator to CPAP but with his alarm sounding that frequently, she started to wonder if it had been done too soon. he had been put on antibiotics today, she knew, so it seemed as if there were problems all round.

Sarah was over there now, conferring with the nurse and checking baby, monitors and chart.

Changing Teresa's nappy through the ports of the isolette, Jennifer couldn't focus any more on what was happening around Daniel Wright's isolette, but there was clearly something going on. She lifted Teresa's little bottom gently, whisked out the wet nappy, wiped with a pre-moistened disposable towelette, then tucked the new nappy into place—all rather efficiently these days. The nurses had been letting her do this job for some weeks now.

She had time to think about Daniel Wright's parents and was thankful in a way that they'd gone home an hour ago and weren't witnessing this new drama over their baby. She could see Sarah bagging air into tiny Daniel now, squeezing the baby with one large hand while she bent to listen to the bird-like chest with her stethoscope. She must have intubated him, preparatory to putting him back on the ventilator.

It was the sort of setback that would have had Jennifer falling apart over Teresa. Again, perhaps, it was good that the Wrights weren't here. Things would be stable again by morning. . .

Except that I always wanted to be here at those crisis times for Teresa, she thought, so I could will her to live and comfort her, if she would take it. She smiled down at her baby, who *would* live now. . .

She looked up again, wide-eyed, when Sarah appeared, her normally strong voice a whisper. 'Jennifer, you've got to help. Baby wright's getting bluer by the minute.' She rattled off some numbers and a technical description of his condition—low on oxygen saturation, blue extremities, heart rate dipping significantly below one hundred beats per minute. 'And I don't know why.'

'But. . .me?'

'Don't argue.' She twisted her large hands. 'There isn't time. I can't page Will,' she continued feverishly. 'I don't want him to know. Or anyone important.' She broke off. 'Kyle's already been threatening to—Oh, hell, Jennifer! Just come!'

CHAPTER NINE

JENNIFER went.

Sarah was visibly shaken and panicked, and the nurse working with Daniel Wright tonight was one of the less experienced staff members in the unit who was covering for a more senior staffer who'd had vacation time owing.

It wasn't Jennifer's baby and this wasn't her job, but all she could think of was that this was the mistake she'd been so afraid Sarah would make on Teresa and it didn't sound as if there was time to fight Sarah's refusal to summon Will or any other senior doctor.

'Still blue. I'm bagging him. It doesn't feel right,' Nurse Chiara Stout summarised in a panicky voice.

'You've tubed him into his stomach instead of his lungs,' Jennifer said to Sarah, almost before she reached the bedside. She had been running through the possibilities like lightning in her mind and this was the only thing that made sense.

But Sarah shook her head. 'No! Surely not! I listened, and it sounded right. I mean, he was hell to tube in the first place. He's a real FLK.'

Not standard medical terminology in anyone's book, this abbreviation, but used widely all the same. It stood for Funny-Looking Kid. Jennifer didn't like the expression, but it could be useful.

In this case, as Sarah pointed out, he had no chin. She went on, 'The angle was terrible. But I got it in and I listened—'

'Sarah, you know with such a small baby you could be listening over the chest and still get the air sounds clear as a bell if they were coming from the stomach,' Jennifer said.

'But surely—! It sounded exactly the same as it always does. Those sounds. . .I mean, God, diagnosing by sound— it's so primitive!' she wailed.

'It *has* to be that!'

Daniel was fighting for his life, and weakly at that. Jennifer didn't waste any more time. She pulled out the tube and turned to Sarah. 'Try again.'

'*You* try! I won't be able to do it. I know I won't!'

'OK. . .' She tried, and it was as hard as Sarah had said. She finally got it, started bagging and listening and it did sound nice and clear in the chest. But Daniel was still blue and only a few precious minutes away from brain damage, and when she listened over the stomach she knew she'd done the same as Sarah.

'We've got to page Will!' she told the other doctor urgently.

'No. . .'

'We've got to!'

'Kyle's on. He's around somewhere.'

'We have to, Sarah, or this baby is going to die. You're right, he's a Funny-Looking Kid. He's hard to tube, for some reason, and Will has the expertise to—'

Sarah was still shaking her head. Jennifer pulled out the tube again and said to the nurse, 'Give him mouth-to-mouth and CPR till Dr Hartman gets here.' She yelled at Allie Briscoe, who was over by the phone, 'Page Dr Hartman, stat!' Then she whirled to face the isolette again, shaking off questioning frowns from three other nurses nearby and ignoring the shocked stares of two mothers who were still with their own babies.

'I'm. . .I'm not having very much luck with this,' Chiara Stout said, her voice high and tense. 'He's so tiny. If I break something. . .'

'I'll try and tube him again,' Jennifer said, grabbing the equipment and trying to remember everything she'd ever learned or read about this—everything she'd seen done or had done herself. At what angle should she have the baby's head? 'Less flexed, maybe,' she muttered.

But Sarah was saying with angry urgency, 'No, Jennifer, not like that, surely! To get past that weird jaw he's got. . .'

Will was here. Jennifer knew of it first from Chiara's fervently breathed, 'Oh, thank God!'

Then Sarah began to stammer miserably, 'I couldn't. . .I couldn't. . .'

He simply cut across all this with only what was necessary. 'Here, Jennifer. Let me. You're still flexing the head too much.'

With one deft series of movements he had done it, tubing with his right hand and bagging with his left so that with miraculous swiftness the ominous blue tone of the baby's skin began to change to a healthy pink, first on his torso and then radiating outwards to the little limbs.

With equal expertise he now detached the manually worked 'ambu-bag' and attached the ventilator, watching the illuminated numbers on its electronic read-out as they steadied. Tiny Daniel's oxygen saturation was rising, and he was taking about every third breath on his own, with the machine doing the rest.

Only now did Will turn to Sarah, saying curtly, 'What happened? Did you tube him into the stomach?'

Sarah had been hunched awkwardly, her face twisted and her top lip raw from where her bottom teeth were gnawing at it. Now she buried her face in her hands. 'I—

Yes, I tubed him wrong. I didn't even realise. *Jennifer* had to tell me. I—I hate this. I can't do it any more. I can't be with patients. I hate them! I want to be in a lab. When Jennifer started putting Baby Fugitt's stomach feed into his IV that was my fault, too, Will. I—I didn't tell you the whole story. I let her take the blame. I just can't practise medicine.'

'It's OK, Sarah,' he told her quietly. 'Go home. We'll talk about this when you're calmer. Tomorrow.'

'I'm sorry, Will. I'm sorry. . .' She broke into ragged sobs and turned to leave, fending off any attempts to stop her. A minute later she had left the unit.

There were several startled, curious or perturbed faces turned in their direction—nurses, parents and Kyle Reeve, who was now dealing with another far more routine crisis several yards away. In a place like this crises tended to happen very publicly, and unless people were certain they could help they generally stayed out of it.

'As you were, everyone,' Will said with calm authority. 'The baby's fine, and Dr Jamieson needs to rethink her career a little.' Then, more privately, he said, 'Jennifer?'

'Yes?'

'Let's talk, shall we?'

'We need to, I think,' she agreed.

By instinct, it seemed, they returned to Teresa, who was sleeping peacefully under the charge of a newer nurse in the unit, Cathy Hong. As Cathy also had four other babies to oversee this evening, though, she wasn't by the familiar isolette at the moment but was changing an IV syringe a little distance away.

'She's gaining nicely again,' Will commented rather absently as they both looked at the baby.

'She is,' Jennifer agreed.

There were some furnishings in the little plastic home these days—a couple of cards with black and white patterns on them which Teresa loved to study, and a plastic teddy bear which was easily washable and not likely, as a plush toy would be, to harbour germs. Jennifer still had Heather's old teddy in her motel room, which would become Teresa's when she was bigger and discharged from the unit.

That goal was getting closer. Next week, if all went well, she would graduate to an open bassinet and would start to wear clothes for the first time. Doll's clothes, actually, because even the preemie sizes were still too big for her.

'Was that right, what Sarah said?' Will asked. 'Was the mix-up over Baby Fugitt's feed syringes her fault?'

'Largely, yes,' Jennifer admitted warily. She had started to assume that Will and Sarah were involved, but it was dawning on her now that there had been little that was lover-like in his response to the other woman tonight. Not yet certain about this, she continued, still with caution, 'I—I have to say I was shocked when she didn't tell you that at the time.'

'But why didn't *you* tell me?' he demanded. 'You just took the blame.'

'Because I *was* to blame in part. You were right. I shouldn't have let Sarah bulldoze me into an inappropriate and ill-thought action. Like tonight—'

'You saved a baby's life tonight, Jennifer.'

'No! How? *You* were the one who finally got him tubed.'

'Because you realised what was wrong and called me in time. Sarah wouldn't have. Kyle Reeve came to see me yesterday about a mistake he'd prevented her making and told me he's covered her on-call four times over the past month. She's falling apart.'

'You must have known she was having a hard time.

You've. . .been seeing a lot of her.' She couldn't help the reproach and accusation that crept into her tone, and he picked up on it, of course, glancing at her sharply across the isolette that separated them.

'Of course I knew she was having a hard time,' he answered. 'And that was *why* I've been seeing such a lot of here.'

'I thought that was because you thought she was good, and because you were inv—'

'She *is* good,' he cut in, 'in that she has a very, very bright mind that would be a major asset to any research team. That was why she was accepted into this residency despite the less-than-glowing reports from her internship rotations. It was generally felt that if she could get through this she'd move into research and be outstanding at it, but nobody realised quite how disastrously she handled patients and pressure.

'She won't be able to stay in the programme now, of course. I doubt she wants to, anyway, from what she said tonight. I'm going to have to call in a favour or two, but I'm hoping to get her into a university research team somewhere where she won't have to have patient contact and where her ability with statistics and analysis will be of real use.'

'Of course,' Jennifer managed. 'You wouldn't want to let her down. You want her to be successful.'

'Yes, I do,' he agreed, 'because it'll be a waste of her mind if she isn't. I also want you to be, which is partly why I'm thanking you rather than bawling you out for what you did tonight.'

'You mean getting involved—again—with a baby who's not my business?'

'Yes.'

'How could I help it, Will, when every baby in the unit—

almost every baby—is as precious to someone as Teresa is to me? Even Kenny Fugitt has his new adoptive parents now, who laugh and cry over every advance and every setback. You said yourself that Daniel Wright wouldn't have lived—'

'I know. You couldn't help what you did. It's deeply ingrained in you. You have to get back to medicine, Jennifer, because you're too good a doctor for the profession to lose you.'

Their eyes met, his grave and dark and carefully distant and hers brimming with the love she felt for him but couldn't show or even trust.

'Thanks, Will,' she said, then her gaze faltered and fell away.

'You ready to wake her for her feed, Jennifer?' Cathy Hong asked, coming over.

'Mmm.' She nodded brightly.

Teresa was still too immature to waken herself reliably through hunger, and needed the artificial schedule in order to keep her gaining steadily.

Will took Nurse Hong's words as his cue to depart, not even saying goodbye—just clucking his tongue at her and giving half a wink. He'd be in and out of the unit tomorrow, apparently, no doubt spending a fair bit of time sorting out the mess over Sarah's dropping out. Then on Saturday he was off, and if Teresa did well enough to earn her discharge during the two weeks he was away.

Jennifer's stomach turned over and she felt sick. That casual wink might be the closest thing she'd get to a goodbye from him. It felt painful, horrible and wrong, and the worst thing was that he didn't seem to realise that they might barely see each other again. Sarah's sensible words about power balance and heroworship returned to her again, seeming more truthful and plausible than ever.

The way she'd fallen on him more than once—needed him so obviously and responded so willingly to his touch—how could he *not* have reacted the way he had? That was all he'd ever felt for her—a flattered pleasure at her evident admiration and faith, which had translated into a brief flaring of attraction.

What a fool I've been, she thought miserably, to let this grow.

Like an opportunistic infection, it seemed to her medical mind, taking root in her because of her turmoil over Teresa. If she'd been less emotional she might have been able to resist, the way a healthy immune system resisted the growth of bacteria.

Which was a far more graphic and morbid comparison than she could possibly be happy with.

Jennifer sorted her dirty clothes into their usual piles in Will's basement and started the first load, then stood there as the water level crept up over jeans and skirts, blouses and the long-sleeved cotton tops she now needed to wear on chilly mornings.

It was a mindless task, watching laundry washing. The water reached its mark and the agitator started its busy, grumbling movement back and forth, sucking the clothes under, covering them with suds and sending them up again.

She sighed. You really couldn't go on watching. It became a form of obsessive insanity.

She looked around Will's basement. He hadn't tidied it. His cleaning service probably vacuumed down here occasionally, but the boxes were still piled in a corner and the exercise bike was getting positively felted with dust. Briefly she considered cleaning it, but soon decided against it. He would notice and consider it pathetic, which it was.

She probably should have stopped coming here weeks ago, when she'd first realised that her feelings for him were getting so out of control, but that might have been worse in a way because the arrangement was so convenient. It would have seemed odd if she'd suddenly discontinued it.

He had been as good as his word, too, and she'd never encountered him here. Or, she amended to herself now, encountered only reminders of him.

That was why she so often just put the load into the machine and went for a walk, returning to fill the dryer and put on a second load before heading off again. Probably he wouldn't have minded if she'd sat on his couch or in the garden and read a book, or even helped herself to coffee and a snack, but because she *wanted* to do those things so much—to be part of his life even in such a mundane way— she didn't let herself.

Today his presence seemed particularly strong here for some reason, and when she'd finally stopped watching that churning load of clothes and closed the lid of the machine she looked up and noticed that the door of the laundry chute which funnelled down from the upstairs bathroom was open and his clothes were falling out of it.

That was where her sense of him was coming from. The clothes spilled their scent, a seductive and too familiar mixture of musky aftershave and hospital soap with the lightest nuance of well-showered male thrown in.

Before she fully realised what she was doing she had reached out and pulled at the blue shirt sleeve that was dangling from the half-open door, then buried her face in the soft folds.

But it brought only the pointless pain of yearning for him, as well as a realisation that this was both foolish and dangerous, so she quickly stuffed the shirt back into the cupboard against the weight of the rest of the clothes piled there and closed the door.

Definitely time to go for that walk!

She clattered quickly up the wooden stairs, pushed open the door into the kitchen and hurried through. . .then almost catapulted into Will's arms as he came through the front door.

It was a horrible moment.

If he had found her in the basement it wouldn't have been so bad, or even if she had been leaving with her arms full of clean, folded clothes. Like this, though, she felt like a trespasser, and if he smelt his own scent on her and guessed that she'd been embracing his shirt. . .!

'You're home,' she blurted unnecessarily.

He smiled, but his humour was a little forced. 'Do I need to apologise?'

'N-no, of course not. I was going for a walk. . .while my things were in the wash. But. . .' She laughed uncomfortably. 'Hey, you're right, it's your house.'

'Your stuff's still in the machine?'

'Yes.'

'Because I've just ducked home to do mine so I can pack tonight. My flight to Boston leaves at seven-thirty tomorrow morning.'

'Oh, you're going to Boston for your vacation?' Her home town.

'No, Nova Scotia. There's a small music festival, and I'll be doing a fair bit of fishing and hiking, too. But, of course, I can't fly direct from Columbus. I connect in Boston.'

'Right. . .'

'So I don't have a lot of time.'

'In Boston? No, I expect—'

'Before I have to be back at the hospital,' he clarified carefully, and she felt stupid for having misunderstood.

'Sorry. If I'd known you were coming. . .'

'Or if *I'd* known *you* were,' he pointed out. 'Look, is it a full load you've got on?'

'No, just medium.'

'Then do you mind if I top it up with my stuff?'

It was a very sensible arrangement, of course, and was carried out quite quickly. She went back into the basement with him and turned a knob or two to raise the water level and lengthen the washing time while he quickly sorted his things into darks and lights, adding the latter to her pile which was sitting on top of the dryer.

'They smell of the perfume you use.'

The caressing words came as she added more liquid detergent to the machine, and she spilled a drop or two on her hand as she looked up, startled. It was so exactly what she had thought about his shirt. Colour flooded her cheeks.

'It's not perfume,' she answered clumsily. 'It's just soap. Sandalwood soap. I didn't want to overwhelm Teresa with chemical scents. I wanted her to know the smell of me.'

The smell of *you* is wonderful,' he murmured.

What happened next was inevitable, perhaps. They both swayed closer to each other, both took a step and that was all that was needed. His arms slid fluidly around her shoulders and he bent his face to hers, tilting his head a little so that his quest for her mouth was swiftly and easily completed.

She had lifted her own face willingly, instinctively closing her eyes so that the first touch of his mouth came just a tiny bit later than she was expecting, which gave it an added magic. It was like biting into a ripe berry when each nodule is so tautly packed with juice that it takes a moment for the berry to burst and release its sweetness.

When that expected and hungrily wanted touch did come, though, it sent immediate tendrils of sensation all through her like hot wires, and she felt her breasts tighten and the secret core of her melt and swell. Her heart began to beat faster and her breathing quickened, and she *wanted* him— with such a painful, wonderful hunger that she was soon lost in it.

'Oh, Will. . .'

He must be able to feel how she was trembling, and if he looked closely he would see the wetness of tears, glistening on her lashes.

This was too hard. It wasn't fair that something could feel so strong and yet mean so little—to one of them, at least. Kissing her like this. . .trailing his mouth over her face to her ear. . .burying himself in her neck, groaning as he cupped her buttocks with lavishly caressing hands. . . During all this he should be talking about love and making promises to her—vowing to cherish her and this feeling between them for ever.

These were the things *she* wanted to say. She had to bite them back, fight to keep from saying them as she was fighting her tears.

He was touching her breasts now through her blouse, stroking along their undersides where the soft, swelling flesh met her ribs and then coming up to cup them and find the aching evidence of her nipples with his thumbs. During this, he should have been telling her he loved her, instead of. . .

'I'm sorry, Jennifer, I have no right. . . This isn't what you need, and it's my fault. It's up to me to call a halt and I keep failing you in that.'

He was shaking, too, she suddenly realised, and the fact shocked her. What was he thinking? What was he feeling? What was he struggling against?

But, no, she knew. Sarah had said it all. The honour that was so strong in him was determined to win over a very primitive male instinct to take what was offered and damn the consequences, and she couldn't blame him for this latter instinct without accepting her own involvement. She wasn't exactly sending him signals to stay clear, with her straining nipples and swollen mouth. Neither was she in a position to make demands when what she felt was built on the quicksand foundation of her emotional vulnerability right now.

So she was in his arms, and neither of them could stop, apparently, despite the fact that they both knew it was necessary. His hands seared to her waist again and then down to her thighs to pull her against the hard evidence of his arousal, and her hips seemed to move wantonly of themselves in a sinuous figure of eight because the feeling of his thighs pressing against her was so wonderful.

His mouth was forcing her neck to arch as his kiss became deeper and more demanding, and she mewed in protest even as she touched her tongue to his and parted her lips further to taste more of him.

Finally, he was the one to gain the necessary strength of Will. Will. . . Yes, he was aptly named, she decided, loving the word.

'This *has* to stop, Jennifer.'

He broke away, suddenly and completely, and she saw that he was panting and his temples were damp. A shudder of repressed need rippled through him, and there was a haunted hollowness to his face. A tortured fire in his dark eyes, too.

'It has to,'; he said. 'I'm going away tomorrow. Two weeks. It sounds like for ever at the moment, and yet I'm not sure that it will be long enough. When I get back—'

'Don't say it, Will!' she begged him, staring down at her fingers through blurred vision. 'Don't! It's not necessary.'

Two weeks for her to get used to the unit without him, and by the end of that time, with any luck, Teresa would be discharged and then—because he was right, two weeks would not be nearly long enough—she would start to forget him and get on with her life.

'I think it is,' he was saying.

'No,' she insisted, 'it's not. I understand. I'd rather just. . . Actually. . .' she forced a laugh '. . .I'd like some fresh air. I was about to go for a walk when you. . .turned up. You probably have other packing to do so let's not talk any more. Difficult words can make such bad memories.'

'OK,' he answered slowly. 'OK, Jennifer. Go for your walk, then.'

'And please let's not say goodbye.'

'No. If you'd prefer.'

'Leave the rest of your laundry if you need to get back to the hospital. I'll finish mine, then put yours in the dryer when I leave.' She saw him hesitate and added desperately, 'Please! So we don't have to. . .cross paths here over our wretched socks!'

'Sure,' he nodded. 'Sure, Jennifer.'

She fled, found the park that opened off an easement a few streets from his house and walked there for a couple of hours until she was certain he'd be safely back at the hospital. Returning to his house, she saw that his car was gone from the driveway and so she dared to go in and deal with her laundry. . .and his.

*   *   *

'Guess where you're going tomorrow?' Helen Bradwell crooned to Teresa as she put the baby back in her isolette after her daily weighing. 'Just guess, little girl, just guess! You're going into an open bassinet. Your mummy is going to be able to kiss you and dress you and pick you up when she wants. She's going to call you Mommy, right?' she asked Jennifer, looking up.

'It's a scary word, but what else?'

'You're right, it is a scary word,' Helen agreed, 'but you'll do great, honey, and you know it.'

'If love and thought and time are enough. . .'

'What else is there? Hey, baby Terri, what else is there?'

Will had been gone for a week now, and Teresa was almost at the magic four-pound mark when Jerry Gaines, in Will's absence, had decreed that she'd be ready to go. Against that approaching deadline Jennifer had been shopping madly—car-seat, bassinet, stroller, lambskin, sheets and quilt and swaddling blankets, nappy bag, clothes, toiletries, medicines and thermometer.

Room 143 at the Sunnyside Motel was getting crowded and she hadn't even begun on the less necessary purchases yet, like a mobile to hang above the bassinet, a music-box playing a lullaby, baby toys.

Everyone told her how excited she must be, and how she probably couldn't wait. Everyone told her how scared she was, too, of course, but how she'd get used to it and become an expert at it sooner than she would imagine possible.

Everyone told her that, of course, she'd probably never want to set foot in this unit again and would want to forget the very existence of the place as soon as she could, but still please to drop a line once in a while and a photo of the baby to let them know how she was doing, and so they could add the photo to their pinboard of 'graduates' which so encouraged parents who'd just plunged into their own difficult time here.

Everyone said all this, but Jennifer felt that none of it was true.

She *wasn't* excited, she *could* wait and she wasn't scared—she was just quietly prepared and determined not to panic. She *didn't* want to forget the very existence of the unit. She wanted to work in one—with new knowledge, understanding and compassion—when she restarted her residency. She wanted to forget Will enough to lose this pain of missing him, yet she wanted to remember him because of what he'd done for Teresa—and for herself, too, in getting her through this.

And lastly, and very foolishly—despite what he'd said himself about her having these two weeks to start preparing for the loss of him in her life—she desperately wanted him to be back before Teresa was discharged so she could see him one more time.

As the second week of his vacation ticked by, however, it became clear that this wasn't going to happen.

Teresa was retaining body heat beautifully in her open bassinet, wearing a tiny wrap-around T-shirt and a little knitted cap and swaddled in a pastel-striped flannel blanket. She was off the apnoea monitor, off the heart monitor and gaining muscle tone. On Wednesday she tipped the scales at 1820 grams, which translated to just a fraction over four pounds.

'We're going to send her home with you on Friday,' Jerry Gaines promised, with the air of bestowing a great gift—which he was, of course, and it was unfair of her to question his wide smile. 'Now, would you like a night in our rooming-in suite first?'

'Yes, please,' she answered promptly, thinking he meant Friday night. Was Will fronting up for work on Saturday? She wasn't sure, and didn't want to ask.

The rooming-in suite was a special section of the unit furnished like a small apartment, where parents could spend their baby's last night in hospital, looking after him or her, with staff easily within each but not summoned unless needed. This could give confidence a big boost but Jennifer wasn't convinced she really needed it, and when she discovered that Jerry had meant Thursday night.

'Maybe there are other parents, though, who—'

'No one else is going to be ready for discharge Friday,' he told her, then insisted expansively, 'Take it!'

So she did, and discovered that confidence in theory was a far different thing from confidence in practice. With no wonderfully experienced nurses, no monitors, no one's judgement but her own. . .

Was Teresa still breathing? Was she warm, contented, fed?

Jennifer checked her about forty zillion times, and slept for a total of three badly disjointed hours herself. Then Friday arrived and, with a last flourish of hospital protocol and paperwork, Teresa was ready to be strapped into her new car-seat and ferried to her new bassinet in Room 143 of the Sunnyside Inn.

It was one of the happiest and one of the most miserable days of Jennifer's life.

CHAPTER TEN

CHECK-OUT time at the Sunnyside Inn was noon, which gave Jennifer and Teresa plenty of time for a Sunday morning walk in the Whetstone Park of Roses beforehand.

It was a glorious autumn day, the first week of October, and the leaves were beginning to turn. The roses were still flowering, though. Apricot Nectar and French Lace, Queen Elizabeth and Tiffany. Teresa, well swaddled in her new quilted sleeping-bag and resting in her stroller on her new lambskin, evidently wasn't particularly interested in roses, however, because she slept through the entire experience until wakened at ten for a feed in the mild sunshine, snuggled blissfully in Jennifer's arms.

The last two nights in the motel had been somewhat less terrifying than that first one in the hospital's rooming-in suite. She had slept with the baby beside her, aware of new research which suggested that proximity to a breathing adult could prompt an infant to breathe and reduce the risk of Sudden Infant Death Syndrome, and this had allowed her to relax more. She had woken Teresa on a four-hourly schedule for feeds, and that had worked out well, too, although she planned to continue two-hourly feeds during the day for a while yet.

This was the last bottle of Kathy Solway's milk, however, which was sad. Jennifer had picked it up on Friday morning, just before Teresa's discharge, and she and Kathy had said a rather emotional goodbye to each other and had

177

promised to keep in touch as they'd become good friends over the past three months.

Teresa would have to start on formula now. Jennifer didn't like the idea but there seemed little choice unless she could locate a willing donor in Boston.

There was so much to think about, so much to do, and wakeful nights to look forward to for the next few months. It would set her apart from her friends, who were all doctors or dancers, all childless and all busy with careers and relationships. She wondered, suddenly, whether she really had a reason to go back to Boston.

To be out here in the open air with Teresa, though, was sheer joy on such a gorgeous day. Grandmotherly ladies peeped at the baby and smiled. Children commented candidly, 'She's so small!' And Jennifer's heart gushed with love like the fountain, gushing in amongst the roses.

There was a lot of packing to do, however, and Teresa should not be tired by too extensive an outing. They mustn't stay long. Back at the motel a little later, Teresa fussed for a few minutes then slept again while Jennifer tackled her task, folding clothes carelessly. She came upon Will's jug-shaped vase and held it in her hand, at a loss. Take it? Yes, but how should she pack it? Stuffed with socks, perhaps, and wedged in amongst blouses and jeans.

A knock sounded at the door while she still had the vase in her hand and she went to answer it, expecting to have to tell Housekeeping that she wasn't yet ready to have the room cleaned.

But it was Will.

He didn't want to be invited in, just lunged forward and kicked the door shut behind him. 'You're packing,' he said accusingly.

'Yes. Ch-check-out time is noon.' She was overwhelmed

by the unexpected sight of him, flustered and happy and aching all at the same time—to the point where she could barely look at him, let alone meet his eye.

'You're not leaving. You *can't* leave!' he said with rough disbelief and desperate authority. 'When I came back yesterday to find she'd already been discharged and you'd gone—' He broke off.

Startled by his anger, she attempted to placate him by explaining her plans. 'I'm going to take it slowly, over three or four days, to make sure she's not tired by the journey. If she doesn't seem to be handling it I'll just stay put in Pennsylvania somewhere for a few days.'

'Ah, hell, Jennifer, I'm not thinking about Teresa!' he rasped.

He was pacing the room now, his dynamism magnetic, making it almost impossible for her to stay away from him. She just had to keep looking down—away—and she folded her arms across her chest to hide the fact that her whole body was aching to touch him.

'I'm thinking about you. . .us,' he was saying.

'*Us*?'

'I thought you understood.'

She laughed shakily. 'I—I don't think I understand anything. I *know* I don't! Everything has been such a mess for me over the past few months. You know that, Will,' she pleaded.

'Yes. Yes. . .' The light of certainty and command had gone out of him now. 'Perhaps I shouldn't have come.'

'But I'm glad you did,' she answered him, trying to put an aura of civility and convention over this, 'because I never thanked you for everything you did for Teresa. I know you'll say it's only what you would have done for any baby in the unit, but—'

'Yes,' he cut in, 'it's what I'd have done, and what I *do* do for any baby, but you're wrong if you think she's not special. She's incredibly special to me, Jennifer, and she has been almost from the beginning—because she's yours.'

Their eyes met. His were smouldering and dark beneath his arrowing brows, and she couldn't believe what she saw reflected there. It was more than desire, wasn't it? 'Will—'

He crossed the space between them and pulled her commandingly into his arms to stare down at her face just inches from his. The strength of his gaze held her, captured her own regard so that she couldn't look away even though she knew he was trying to read her to her very depths.

'Listen,' he said urgently. 'All along, this has been an impossible situation. You've been the parent of a patient and you've been acutely vulnerable and prone to wildly swinging emotions. I've known that. I've seen it so much with so many people in our unit, and they didn't have the death of a sister to deal with on top of the rest. I've known it's been the worst possible time in your life to ask you to even *know* what you're feeling, let alone to *trust* it.

'For all those reasons I've tried to hold back, to wait until our relationship wasn't complicated by professional. . .or even ethical. . .issues, and I thought you understood I was doing that. But now, today, to find that you're on the point of leaving, as if you don't want to follow this through. . .'

'Follow it through. . . Follow what through, Will? Are you saying—?

'That I love you, of course,' he muttered darkly as he grazed her mouth. 'I can't ask you to tell me today that you feel the same. I know that. There just can't be room in your heart for you to know yet whether you do or you don't, but surely you feel enough to stay here in Columbus—to stay with me and find out. Jennifer, I *won't* lose you because of bad timing and bad circumstances. What I feel is too strong. For the first time since Amy, ten years ago, there's a feeling that you *belong* in my life. Even more than she did. Can't we explore this?'

His mouth had grown hungrier and slid along her throat, moving against her lips as he spoke and searing her face. She shuddered and buried her head in his neck. 'Can't we?' he groaned again.

'Yes. Oh, yes. I—I do love you, Will. You nourish me and make me melt in a way that no one ever has before. But I didn't think. . . Sarah said all this stuff to me about power balances and hero worship and vulnerability. It made so much sense. There *were* those things between us. You said as much, didn't you? I felt it in you, and when Sarah and I made that mistake over Kenny Fugitt's feed syringe—'

'There still are those issues. And you're right. I saw it so clearly that night with Baby Fugitt—how dangerous it was to be involved personally when your position in the unit was already so unclear. Which is why we still need to wait,' he urged. 'Perhaps most of what you think you feel is really gratitude, dependence.'

'No!'

'This is too important, Jennifer. You know what a sick baby can do to people's marriages and friendships.'

'That's true. . .'

'So we'll wait. A wonderful wait. Sarah has left a vacant slot in Riverbank's residency programme. You can take it, if you want, and since she's finished her NICU rotation we wouldn't be working together, which I think would be best.'

'It would. But Teresa. . .'

'Helen Bradwell is looking for special needs babies for her home day care.'

'That's right. She told me about it. And I like Helen.'

'So do I. And you couldn't ask for someone who knows Teresa better, other than yourself.'

'But what about *you* and Teresa, Will? Are you saying. . .?'

'I want to be her father. I want you to marry me when we both have a better reason to be sure about this, and a year from now—when she's talking—I want to hear her call me Daddy.'

Tears filled Jennifer's eyes suddenly. 'I don't know why you'd want that—why you'd want to saddle yourself with us. She's not going to be an easy-care baby for quite a long time.'

'That's the only kind I know, my darling. And as for why I want to. . . It began before I even met you when I heard you'd dropped everything in Boston in order to be here with Heather as she was dying. It was the same sort of bombshell I'd had when Amy died during my residency, and you reacted the same way I had, by putting everything else aside. I wanted to save you from burn-out and break-down—at first just for your sake and Teresa's, and then, very selfishly, because I wanted you in my life.

'For a long time a part of me fought it because the way seemed so thick with pitfalls, but then—on the day I first saw your really holding Teresa in your arms—I knew at last that *nothing* would make me give up on this. My God, if I'd been held up at the hospital this morning and you'd already checked out when I got here. . .'

He shuddered and held her tight, pressing his mouth to her hair and then turning her face upwards. They were hungry for each other now. Desperately so. She parted her lips to receive his kiss, then threaded her fingers through his hair and held him to her while they moved feverishly together, his hands pressing her hips against his so that his arousal was blatant.

Interestingly enough, there was a very nice double bed just feet away in a state of inviting disarray, and soon they had fallen onto it. His weight on her was as delicious as she had known it would be—warm, commanding, familiar—crushing her breasts in a way that only made them more alive, more tenderly sensitive. And when he slid his hands beneath her blue embroidered chambray shirt and began to caress her she gasped and arched with delight.

The knock at the door didn't even penetrate their awareness, but when they both heard the sound of the lock clicking back. . .

It wasn't a convincing performance. A man and a woman just didn't perch on the edge of a motel bed as prim and upright as strictly disciplined schoolchildren in the middle of the day. The woman from Housekeeping who had been cleaning Jennifer's room for three months, and who had spent fifteen minutes clucking over Teresa yesterday, had evidently seen it all before.

'Oh, you're not ready, doll?' Marie said comfortably. Then she grinned. 'You might like to know that there's a special check-out option for long-term guests like you. You don't need to be out by noon. One or two o'clock is fine. You won't be charged for another day.'

Then she took another look at them. 'Or make that three o'clock. If you really need it.'

'Thanks,' Will growled. 'But, actually, we'd better call the front desk because there's been a change of plan. She's not checking out today after all.'

'Oh, she isn't?' Marie beamed, took an even closer look

and grinned. 'Congratulations, doll. I hope you'll both be very happy.

'This is your baby brother, darling,' Jennifer said to the blonde-haired, brown-eyed three-year-old girl who had just entered the hospital room.

Teresa was eager but a little awed by the unfamiliar place, despite the hour-long 'Prepared Sibhood' session she had done here at the hospital two weeks earlier with Mommy and Daddy. She had her hand stretched up to hold Daddy's, and at first he had to coax her into the room. But when she saw the bundle of blanket in Mommy's arms. . .

Jennifer winced a little as Teresa climbed awkwardly onto the bed to get a closer look. She had given birth just two hours earlier, at five past three in the afternoon, and was still, to say the least, distinctly sore. But pain and discomfort were amazingly easy to ignore under the circumstances.

'He's got lots of hair,'Teresa said. 'All black. And he's got red skin.'

'Babies all do, love, when they're this little.'

'He *is* little,' Teresa agreed seriously. 'He's tiny!'

In fact, compared to Teresa two hours after *her* birth, he was huge, having weighed in at a more than respectable eighth and a half pounds. Obstetrician Richard Gilbert, himself now the father of two wildly active but very charming little boys just eighteen months apart in age, had said rather smugly, 'Didn't I tell you he'd be big?'

Labour and delivery had been routine and normal on paper, though it had felt anything but routine to Will and Jennifer. He was so used to births that went wrong and babies that came too soon, and she had felt as new at this as the first man in space.

'My experience as a mother doesn't kick in until we get to take the baby home,' she had philosophised to Will early in labour before the contractions got to the point of absorbing all her energy and focus. It had been pretty intense there for a while, until she'd experienced the miracle of having Stephen laid in her arms. Now all that was behind her.

So much was behind her.

'Can I hold him on my lap, Mommy?' Teresa said, and Jennifer's eyes met Will's over the little girl's head.

'If—if Daddy helps, love,' she said hesitantly. 'And if you're very, very careful.'

Teresa was three and a half years old now. She had needed no more eye surgery but still wore glasses, currently with the left lens frosted to strengthen the weaker right eye. Her intelligence seemed clear—she was curious, creative and quite a chatterbox—but her motor skills were not quite so good and she could be clumsy and weak-muscled in some tasks. An Olympic sporting medal was unlikely in her future.

Jennifer's instinct, therefore, was to panic at the thought of her holding Stephen. With the legacy of her experience with Teresa's fragility it was hard not to be over-protective, but she knew that this first meeting between the three-year-old and her baby brother was so important in setting the tone for their future relationship.

'I'm sure he'd love to have his big sister holding him,' she appended to her initial slightly doubtful statement.

Teresa beamed, and her brown eyes lit up behind her glasses. When she smiled she was a gorgeous little elf, still small for her age and very fine of feature.

She's so precious! Jennifer thought. Her heart turned over as she watched Will tenderly settle her into a chair and pack pillows on her lap before he came over to pick up Stephen, who was awake now and making little faces. Was it fair to give her a brother, who'll be taking attention from her? she wondered inwardly, in a rare moment of doubt.

Ultimately, she knew it *was* fair, though, and confidence returned once more. Her love could easily stretch to encompass two.

This putting of Teresa's interests first was instinctive by this time, and Will shared in it fully. At his suggestion, they had waited a full year before marrying.

'For Teresa's sake,' he had said when they were talking about future plans. 'If it weren't for her I'd marry you tomorrow, but with her in the picture we need to be *more* than sure that we can make this work.'

Jennifer had agreed, and so they had waited and hadn't even lived together until after the wedding.

It hadn't been a particularly onerous separation, though, and really there had never been any doubt. She and Teresa had moved into a two-bedroomed apartment just blocks from Will's house and had spent all their free time there. He had been 'Daddy' to Teresa from the day of their formal engagement.

Then at their wedding, on a sunny September afternoon in the Whetstone Park of Roses, Teresa had given him the best wedding present of all by calling him that quite distinctly just minutes after the ceremony. 'Dadda! Dadda!'

Now it was January two and a half years later. Will's parents, delightful people who were living in retirement in Florida, had come up to mind Teresa at home during the baby's birth, and even Jennifer's parents were expected for a visit some time in the next few weeks. Jennifer intended to make the situation quite clear at that point.

Julia and Walter Powell had been delighted at Jennifer's marriage to Will and had embraced their role as Teresa's grandparents adequately if not effusively of late, but they still had a distance to go to achieve Mr and Mrs Hartman's degree of warmth.

'There will be no favouritism,' Jennifer had vowed to Will, 'and I'll tell them so if I have to. If they can't love Teresa as much as the new baby then they won't get to see either of them.'

'Harsh?' Will had queried.

'Necessary!'

'You know what you want, sweetheart, don't you?'

'And I know what I have to do to get it!'

It was a trait that might come in handy a year and a half from now when, after a period of maternity leave and part-time work, Jennifer would be fully qualified and ready to pursue her goal of partnership in a paediatric practice.

But professional ambition was not uppermost in her mind at the moment. Teresa had Stephen safely on her lap now, and her little face was ablaze with a rapt, elfin grin. Will was crouching beside the chair, ready to head off any mishap before it could even begin to occur, and his face was as bright as his adopted daughter's, with the added complexity of an adult's love reflected there.

It made the most wonderful picture Jennifer had ever seen, she thought, her eyes beginning to mist.

There was snow on the ground the day you were born, Stephen, beautiful white snow, she rehearsed, knowing she'd want to tell her new baby the story of his birth, in the same way that she'd started to tell Teresa the story of hers. *Your Daddy and I were so happy when it came time to go to the hospital in the middle of the night because we knew that you were ready to come out of my tummy and we were going to get to meet you soon. But we were a little scared we'd get stuck on the slippery roads in the snow. We didn't get stuck, though, because your daddy is a very good driver. . .*

And a good doctor, a good husband and a *very* good labour coach. They'd both cried after the birth.

These are the two luckiest children in the world, Jennifer decided as she watched the picture that the three of them made, her eyes absolutely swimming with love now. To have such happy parents. . .

Then her eyes met Will's over Teresa's golden head once more, and they smiled at each other across a hospital room that was, at this moment, right next door to heaven.

4 FREE

books and a surprise gift!

We would like to take this opportunity to thank you for reading this Mills & Boon® book by offering you the chance to take FOUR more specially selected titles from the Medical Romance™ series absolutely FREE! We're also making this offer to introduce you to the benefits of the Reader Service™—

- ★ FREE home delivery
- ★ FREE gifts and competitions
- ★ FREE monthly newsletter
- ★ Books available before they're in the shops
- ★ Exclusive Reader Service discounts

Accepting these FREE books and gift places you under no obligation to buy, you may cancel at any time, even after receiving your free shipment. Simply complete your details below and return the entire page to the address below. *You don't even need a stamp!*

YES! Please send me 4 free Medical Romance books and a surprise gift. I understand that unless you hear from me, I will receive 4 superb new titles every month for just £2.30 each, postage and packing free. I am under no obligation to purchase any books and may cancel my subscription at any time. The free books and gift will be mine to keep in any case.

M8XE

Ms/Mrs/Miss/Mr ....Initials ....
BLOCK CAPITALS PLEASE
Surname ....
Address ....

....

....Postcode....................................

Send this whole page to:
THE READER SERVICE, FREEPOST, CROYDON, CR9 3WZ
(Eire readers please send coupon to: P.O. Box 4546, Dublin 24.)

Offer not valid to current Reader Service subscribers to this series. We reserve the right to refuse an application and applicants must be aged 18 years or over. Only one application per household. Terms and prices subject to change without notice. Offer expires 30th September 1998. You may be mailed with offers from other reputable companies as a result of this application. If you would prefer not to receive such offers, please tick box. ☐
Mills & Boon® Medical Romance™ is a registered
trademark of Harlequin Mills & Boon Ltd.

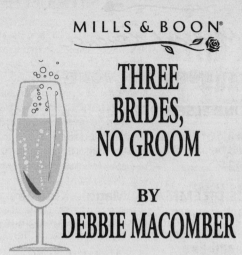

MILLS & BOON®

THREE BRIDES, NO GROOM

BY
DEBBIE MACOMBER

We are delighted to bring you three brand-new stories
about love and marriage from one of our
most popular authors.

Even though the caterers were booked, the bouquets
bought and the bridal dresses were ready to wear...the
grooms suddenly got cold feet. And that's when three
women decided they weren't going to get mad...they
were going to get even!

On sale from 6th April 1998
Price £5.25

*Available at most branches of WH Smith, John Menzies,
Martins, Tesco, Asda, Volume One, Sainsbury and Safeway*

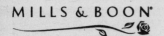

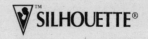

SPECIAL OFFER £5 OFF

FLYING FLOWERS

Beautiful fresh flowers, sent by 1st class post to any UK and Eire address.

We have teamed up with Flying Flowers, the UK's premier 'flowers by post' company, to offer you £5 off a choice of their two most popular bouquets the 18 mix (CAS) of 10 multihead and 8 luxury bloom Carnations and the 25 mix (CFG) of 15 luxury bloom Carnations, 10 Freesias and Gypsophila. All bouquets contain fresh flowers 'in bud', added greenery, bouquet wrap, flower food, care instructions, and personal message card. They are boxed, gift wrapped and sent by 1st class post.

To redeem £5 off a Flying Flowers bouquet, simply complete the application form below and send it with your cheque or postal order to; **HMB Flying Flowers Offer, The Jersey Flower Centre, Jersey JE1 5FF.**

ORDER FORM (Block capitals please) Valid for delivery anytime until 30th November 1998 MAB/0298/A

Title .... Initials .... Surname ....

Address ....

....

.... Postcode ....

Signature .... Are you a Reader Service Subscriber **YES/NO**

Bouquet(s) **18 CAS** (Usual Price £14.99) **£9.99** ☐   **25 CFG** (Usual Price £19.99) **£14.99** ☐

I enclose a cheque/postal order payable to Flying Flowers for £ .... or payment by

VISA/MASTERCARD ☐☐☐☐☐☐☐☐☐☐☐☐☐☐☐☐☐☐ Expiry Date .... / .... /

PLEASE SEND MY BOUQUET TO ARRIVE BY .... / .... / ....

TO Title .... Initials .... Surname ....

Address ....

....

.... Postcode ....

Message (Max 10 Words) ....

....

Please allow a minimum of four working days between receipt of order and 'required by date' for delivery.

You may be mailed with offers from other reputable companies as a result of this application. Please tick box if you would prefer not to receive such offers. ☐

Terms and Conditions Although dispatched by 1st class post to arrive by the required date the exact day of delivery cannot be guaranteed. Valid for delivery anytime until 30th November 1998. Maximum of 5 redemptions per household, photocopies of the voucher will be accepted.